Stanton Thundler has been looking forward to the haunted hay maze ever since his co-worker's boyfriend promised everyone tickets. When he gets there, the place doesn't disappoint. He laughs, screams, and hollers with the rest of his buddies . . . until he lingers over a display too long, takes a wrong turn, and ends up separated from his friends. Stanton doesn't mean to bump into the slender hottie and knock him into a puddle of mud.

Francois Toulouse is irritated when he's ordered to go to a coven near Amarillo and inspect their beef. The only thing he knows about cows is how to cook them so they taste amazing. Then he learns a seer has foreseen that he'll meet his beloved there. The human Fate chooses for him is not what he expects. Stanton is big, brawny, dirty, and a polar opposite to Francois's fastidious tidiness and sophistication. Still, Stanton is his beloved . . .

To Stanton's surprise, Francois asks him out. While he's flattered, he declines. What would be the point when even Stanton can see they have nothing in common?

Navigating the Vampire Maze
Copyright © 2019 Charlie Richards
ISBN: 978-1-4874-2741-2
Cover art by Angela Waters

Published by eXtasy Books Inc or
Devine Destinies, an imprint of eXtasy Books Inc

Look for us online at:
www.eXtasybooks.com or www.devinedestinies.com

Navigating the Vampire Maze
A Loving Nip Book Twenty

By

Charlie Richards

DEDICATION

Life is growth. If we stop growing, technically and spiritually, we are as good as dead.
~Morihei Ueshiba

CHAPTER ONE

Doing his best not to bounce in his seat, Stanton Thundler picked at the fraying knee of his jeans to release the excess energy instead. He stared out the window where he sat in the passenger seat of his best friend's pick-up truck. Anticipation thrummed through him.

"Excited?"

Stanton turned his attention to Jerome, his brows shooting up. "Yeah, I thought—" Then he spotted the twinkle in his bestest buddy's dark eyes as well as the huge grin on his face and realized he was teasing him. Scoffing, Stanton rolled his eyes as he reached over and bumped his fist into Jerome's upper arm. "Dork."

Still grinning, Jerome winked at him.

Appreciating his friend's teasing, Stanton finally gave in to his excitement and began bouncing his leg. "I haven't been to a haunted maze since—" He paused, frowning. His excitement ebbed as he recalled his past.

"That long, huh? Me, too, man." Jerome reached over and patted his thigh. "Awful nice of Rhyme to give us all tickets, isn't it?"

Stanton nodded, appreciating the subject change. He hated thinking about his family. Any time thoughts of his father— *Nope. Not gonna think about him.*

"I looked up how much tickets are to this place," Jerome continued. "He's either loaded or is well-connected with the owners."

Something in Jerome's tone caught Stanton's attention. Did

his friend look concerned? "What do you mean?"

Stanton half-turned in his bucket seat and scratched his shoulder against the backrest. He didn't worry about money too much. Since he shared an apartment with Jerome, his buddy helped him with bills. Stanton wasn't rich by any means, but he met his obligations, and Jerome had even shown him how to budget so he could save money for retirement every month.

"I mean the tickets Max gave everyone at work are all-access. You can ride the hay wagon through the haunted forest, go in the hay maze, and it includes ten game tickets . . . all without paying." Jerome's eyebrows furrowed, and his thick brown lips pinched together in an expression Stanton recognized as worry. "They're sixty-two bucks each."

"Wow. That's a lot of money for an evening of fun." Stanton cocked his head, mulling over what Jerome had told him for a moment as his buddy continued to drive them to the ranch. He didn't get it. "Why would they offer something like that? How much is just access to the haunted hay maze?"

Stanton hadn't been aware that the ranch offered more than that. Of course, after Rhyme had told him he would give all Max's co-workers tickets — those who wanted them anyway — he hadn't looked into it further. Max's boyfriend had assured Stanton that their hay bales were stacked over seven feet high, which meant they would tower over even Stanton's six-foot-five height.

Or is Rhyme Max's partner now that they're living together. Oh, maybe that's why he's being so nice.

Before Stanton could voice his thought, Jerome told him, "The tickets for just the haunted hay maze are twelve bucks."

"Really?"

"Yup. The average time it takes to get through the maze is an hour and twenty minutes. It's huge." Jerome glanced his way before telling him, "And the haunted forest ride takes almost an hour, too. This is a huge operation for them and brings in thousands each October."

"Holy shit," Stanton mumbled. "Guess I should have checked out their website."

Jerome chuckled softly. "On top of that, they have game booths where you can play for stuffed animals or goldfish or other toys, although that's geared mostly for kids." Reaching over, he punched Stanton's upper arm playfully. "Think your beta fish would like a playmate?"

Stanton laughed. "Naw. Billy would eat'em."

As Jerome snorted, Stanton spotted the turn for the ranch. He straightened in his seat and gazed out the window. His concern over Rhyme's motives slipped from his mind as he grinned with excitement.

"Damn, they're busy," he commented as he spotted the dozens upon dozens of vehicles parked in the left field. There were people milling around the edge of the field where a road disappeared between the trees. "Oh, look." Stanton pointed, grinning. "There's the tractor Rhyme mentioned."

Jerome nodded as he turned into the field. Rolling down his window, he waved at Murdoch, who was a friend of Rhyme's and a fellow wrangler. The man appeared to be directing visitors on where to park.

"Hey, Jerome," Murdoch greeted, smiling and tipping his hat in a friendly way. He ducked down a little, allowing the six-foot-one man to see into the cab. "Evening, Stanton." Then Murdoch straightened and pointed to the right. "Vernon and Lloyde arrived just ahead of you. I put them over there with Lilibeth and George. They're still milling around their vehicles, so I figure they're waiting for you."

"Thanks, man," Jerome replied, waving again as he started his truck slowly across the field in that direction.

"Oh, hey." Murdoch jogged the couple of steps to Jerome's open window as he stopped the truck. Resting his tanned hand on the frame, he glanced between them before asking,

"Are Anthony, Benjamin, and Esmerelda still working at your construction company?"

Jerome groaned. "Yeah. Please tell me they aren't here tonight."

Murdoch's lips twisted into a grimace. "Fraid I can't. They arrived thirty minutes ago. If they received the same passes Rhyme gave you all, they could be anywhere by now."

"Thanks for the warning," Jerome stated, shaking his head. "Not sure how they even knew we were coming here tonight."

Shrugging, Murdoch told them, "Rhyme will handle it if you have any trouble with them." Then he backed away, turning toward another vehicle coming up behind them. At the same time, he hollered, "Have fun anyway."

When Jerome began the truck creeping forward again, Stanton admitted, "I told Esmerelda we were coming tonight."

Sometimes, the muscular blonde flirted with him, and Stanton sort of liked it. Didn't everyone like to be flirted with? The woman was beautiful, even if she did hang out with Anthony and Benjamin. The three were known as the homophobe squad.

When Esmerelda rubbed her hand over his arm or shoulder, Stanton's stomach clenched, and his groin warmed. He would fight back a blush as he found an excuse to get away from her. If he didn't, she would continue touching, and his skin would goose bump, or the hairs on his neck would stand on end.

Stanton rarely had that reaction . . . to anyone—male or female. Was it attraction? Going to bars with Jerome, he'd had plenty of people blatantly hit on him, but that was a bar. Stanton knew how to respond to those people, and he'd even occasionally accepted their offers for a backdoor hook-up.

Knowing Esmerelda wasn't a nice person, coupled with

the fact that he worked with her, Stanton didn't really know what to do about it or even what it meant. When she asked questions, he was always polite. He didn't know what else to do.

Maybe that's why Esmerelda flirts with me . . . or maybe she's not flirting, and she's just being nice, too.

"Makes sense that she would ask you," Jerome stated, smirking. "You know if you tap her, she'll leave you alone."

"Tap her? Why would I tap her?" Stanton frowned as he focused on Jerome. Sometimes the man used an expression he just didn't understand. Fortunately, Stanton knew his buddy didn't mind if he bluntly asked for an explanation. "Wait, that means something other than what I think, doesn't it?"

As Jerome parked the truck beside Lloyde's dark-green one, he told Stanton, "If you say you're gonna tap someone, it means you plan to fuck that person."

Stanton grimaced even as he felt his cheeks heat. His stomach twisted. While she'd made his groin warm, he had never once considered fucking her.

In fact, just the thought caused his balls to feel as if they were crawling up into his body.

"Hell, no," Stanton barked, shifting restlessly in his seat. He suddenly needed air. Muttering under his breath, he shoved from the truck. "Never gonna happen." Stanton slammed the door shut.

"Whoa, hey, Stan," Jerome called, following him out of the truck. "I didn't mean to upset you." He rounded the truck at a jog and stopped beside him, placing his hand on Stanton's shoulder and squeezing. "It was a joke."

Stanton clenched his jaw for a second even as he nodded. "Not funny," he mumbled, although he couldn't be certain why the idea of screwing Esmerelda bothered him so much. "She's a bitch."

That has to be it.

"Hey, guys!" Lilibeth called, drawing their attention and

waving in greeting. She grinned broadly as she crossed to them. Grabbing Stanton's arm and wrapping her hand around it, Lilibeth bounced on the balls of her feet as she beamed up at him. "Are you ready for some fun?"

Even though Stanton guessed it was a rhetorical question—Jerome had needed to explain that a couple of times to him—he still nodded. "Yeah."

"Then let's go." Lilibeth started moving, so Stanton fell into step next to her, automatically shortening his long strides so he didn't leave her in the dust. "I just got a text from Max. He and Rhyme saved seats for us on the next tractor ride." She bumped her shoulder into Stanton's lower arm—since that was where her short stature placed her—and grinned up at him. "They knew you'd like that."

Stanton nodded. He would like that. It was nice that his co-worker remembered.

Or is he my friend now?

Stanton knew Jerome was his friend. They'd been friends before they started working together. How could a co-worker turn into a friend?

I'm not sure. Except, Lilibeth is my friend, and I work with her. She invites me places, and we hang out occasionally. Now that Max is doing that, too, that must mean he's my friend, too.

"You okay, Stanton?" Jerome asked, touching the small of his back, drawing his attention. He did that when he knew Stanton had gotten stuck in his head. "Everything all right?"

"Oh, yeah." Stanton grinned at his buddy. "I'm good."

Jerome nodded and smiled, his dark eyes twinkling. "Then let's go have some fun."

Stanton nodded, a grin splitting his lips. "Yeah."

They reached the far end of the pasture turned parking lot, and Stanton spotted Rhyme standing near the foot of the wagon. He smiled widely, his lips pressed together, and waved at them.

As soon as they reached the wagon, Rhyme indicated that

they load up, offering Lilibeth a hand like a gentleman. Stanton followed, and after Lilibeth had given a hug to Max, then settled on a hay bale, Stanton did the same. He spotted George, another co-worker and an all right guy — although his thoughtless mouthy comments sometimes landed him in hot water — sitting a little ways away with his girlfriend, Kristine. Stanton waved, and George lifted his chin in acknowledgement while offering him a grin. Then he went back to paying attention to his girlfriend.

George had met the blonde at the ranch the same weekend Max had met Rhyme. Although, Kristine didn't work at the ranch. In fact, Stanton didn't know where Kristine worked, but they seemed happy together.

Feeling his hay bale jostle a little, Stanton noted that Jerome had plopped down next to him. A moment later, the tractor's engine grew louder as whoever was driving started forward. Stanton felt his excitement grow, and he peered around eagerly.

They followed the narrow track that led into the trees, passing people coming and going. For a few seconds, the only light was that of the tractor's and the flashlights of the walkers . . . if they had one. Then hanging lanterns appeared in the distance, swinging from the boughs of the trees and lighting the way.

After a five minute ride, more lights appeared ahead. The trees thinned. Then Stanton spotted booths between the trunks, benches, and tables for relaxing and eating, and plenty of people of all ages milling around. Many of the people were dressed in costume, but Stanton could easily tell who the workers were, for they were all dressed as Dracula, in black pants, a white shirt with a maroon vest over it, and a black cloak.

Holy shit! They even have fangs!

Stanton had to grin at that. These guys really went all out.

Finally, the tractor passed the booths and cleared the trees, entering another field. This one, however, was dominated by the promised hay maze. Tall torches bracketed the entrance, which had a plank over the top and more hay bales on it to form an arch.

"Wow," Jerome mumbled. "That thing has to stand eight feet high."

"Yeah." Grinning widely, Stanton bounced in his seat. "Let's check it out!"

With Stanton in the lead, the group climbed off the wagon and headed toward the maze. When the female Dracula called, "Tickets, please," Stanton began digging his out of the pocket of his faded jeans.

Rhyme stepped forward and waved. "They're all covered, Shelly."

"Hey, Rhyme." Shelly winked. "Have fun, ya'll."

Stanton nodded as he felt Jerome rest his hand on the small of his back and guide him forward. Five feet into the maze, they reached a T-junction. After a glance at the others, Stanton turned left . . . and almost immediately barked a cry of surprise and lifted his arms in defense as a fake giant spider came soaring toward his head.

Once the hairy arachnid bounced back up on its pulley, disappearing at the top of the hay wall, everyone began to laugh as they moved on.

CHAPTER TWO

"By zee gods, Fate has got to be kidding me."

Francois Toulouse stared up at the huge man who'd just barreled around the corner of the haunted hay maze and knocked him down.

The brawny human sported wide shoulders under his navy blue jacket. His faded and slightly raggedy jeans — there was the start of a hole in his right knee — appeared nearly painted on, showcasing massive thighs and thick calves. The man's huge feet were encased in dirty, dark-brown steel-toed boots.

Being a vampire — stronger and tougher than his whipcord lean six-foot-one frame would make people assume — Francois would normally have blasted the human with a hefty dose of vitriol. Except, when he'd inhaled to do just that, the scent of the man's blood tantalized his taste buds. His fangs suddenly ached with his desire to sink them into the human's vein so he could draw what he knew would be the most delicious blood in the world to flow across his tongue.

"Oh, hey, little man." The big human smiled uncertainly even as he reached out his hand. "I'm sorry. I didn't mean to mow you down. I thought my friends might be around this corner."

As Francois reached out and took the big man's hand, two things hit him at once. First, the wetness along the right side of his right thigh made him wince. Second, when his fingers touched the guy's hand, the hairs on that arm stood on end.

Then the stranger wrapped his fingers around Francois's

and easily hefted him to his feet.

Impressive.

Francois met the man's light-brown eyes while keeping his hold on his hand, ignoring the human's attempt to release him, noticing how work-roughened it felt against his own smooth skin. He rubbed his thumb along the guy's pulse point as he squeezed lightly. At the same time, Francois admired the man's features. He was handsome in a rugged sort of way. His hair was shorn so close to his scalp that, in the low light, Francois wasn't certain just how dark a blond it was.

"It is fine," Francois purred, stepping closer to him. "I am Francois Toulouse. And who would you be, handsome man?"

"Uh—"

The human's eyebrows shot up, and a charming flush darkened his cheeks.

Lovely.

"I'm Stanton. Uh, Stanton Thundler."

Once again, Stanton attempted to pull his hand free. Francois took complete advantage. Ever-so-discreetly, he allowed his claw to slide out just a smidge. When Stanton yanked lightly and Francois released, he scraped that talon across the flesh of his palm, nicking him.

"Oh, ow," Stanton commented mildly as he turned his hand palm up. A bead of blood oozed up near the fleshy base of his thumb. "Damn."

The scent of just that tiny red pearl caused Francois's senses to reel. He barely managed to fight back a moan as his mouth watered. Licking his lips, he swallowed . . . hard.

Only Stanton beginning to lift his hand to his own mouth, probably intending to suck on the wound, drew Francois out of his haze.

"Allow me," Francois purred, snagging Stanton's wrist. "I may have chipped a nail when I fell," he hedged while pulling Stanton's hand toward his own mouth.

To Francois's pleasure, Stanton didn't resist. It was probably mostly due to the confusion mixed with arousal flooding his scent. That was okay. Francois would clear it up eventually.

Francois slid his tongue across Stanton's flesh, lapping up the blood. As the succulent, iron-rich fluid teased his taste buds, he barely resisted the urge to moan. His mouth watered with his need for more, but Francois knew he had to wait.

Hell, Francois had been waiting four days for this human to turn up. A few more hours wouldn't hurt anything.

"You shouldn't lick strangers' hands."

Stanton's confused-sounding warning jerked Francois out of his revelry of his beloved's blood.

And zis big human is my beloved . . . just as zat asshole who visited our coven told me.

For an instant, Francois recalled that day over a week ago.

Francois worked as the chef for a vampire coven in the mountains of Montana. He enjoyed creating new dishes, experimenting with spices, and he ran a tight ship. Everyone, from Master Dante — their coven's leader — to the youngest of children, knew to stay out of his kitchen if he wasn't there to supervise.

The massive kitchen on the ranch was Francois's domain.

"Hey, Francois," Kellan greeted, leaning against the door frame. The vampire second grinned at him. The friendly male's brown eyes twinkled. "Master Dante needs to see you in his office."

Without ceasing in kneading the dough he worked — he planned to make baguettes for tomorrow's breakfast — Francois stared at Kellan with lifted brows. "Zis minute?"

Kellan lifted one shoulder in a half-shrug. "It's important." He waggled his eyebrows. "Trust me."

Francois did trust his vampire second. If Kellan said it was important, then it was. "I must knead zis for anozer minute. I will be zere as quickly as I can."

"I'll let him know." Kellan pushed away from the door frame and turned to leave. "Oh, bring a couple bottles of champagne and half a dozen flutes."

"We are celebrating?"

Kellan grinned broadly. "Oh, yeah."

True to his word, as soon as Francois finished kneading his dough, he prepared to head up to his master's office. As he placed a dish towel over the bowl, then washed his hands, he wondered what they could need him for. The last time Francois had been asked to Master Dante's office, it had been so they could ask him to secretly prepare a cake to celebrate Dante's one hundredth anniversary with his beloved, Ruth.

Francois grabbed a tray, then placed two bottles of champagne and six flutes on it. With the ease of centuries of practice, he easily balanced it on his palm as he exited the kitchen. He made his way up the stairs and stopped at Dante's office.

Before Francois had even knocked, Kellan was opening it. "Nice. Come on in," he said, taking the platter and heading toward the sideboard. "Shut the door."

Obeying, Francois entered and closed the door behind him. As he expected, Dante sat behind his desk, a pleased smile on his lightly tanned features. Francois spotted Karina, too — a female vampire who stood in as the head enforcer when Monte wasn't on this plane of existence. The redheaded vampire was bonded with not only a prairie dog shifter, but also the Horseman of War, so some of the time he resided in the demon realm.

As Francois settled in a chair, he took in the other pair seated in the room. A large male of obvious Native American descent sat on a small sofa with his arm around a lean, toned man. From their scents, the first was a wolf shifter and the second a human . . . and they were a bonded couple.

"Thank you for coming, Francois," Master Dante greeted.

"Of course, Master Dante," Francois replied.

Master Dante used a hand to indicate his guests, saying, "This is Enforcer Carson, from a wolf shifter pack in Colorado, and his mate, Jared." His smile turned amused. "They have come with a message from Seer Laurent."

"Seer Laurent?"

Who zee hell is zat?

Evidently, Dante recognized his confusion, for he continued, "Seer Tim Laurent is mated with a bear shifter, and he saw you." His smile turned understanding. "I had him checked into when Carson and Jared arrived this morning."

The pop of the cork leaving the champagne bottle caused Francois to whip his attention back to Kellan. The second began filling the flutes. No one said anything until he'd handed one to everyone.

Francois had just taken a sip of the bubbly liquid when Master Dante stated, "I'm sending you to a ranch owned by a coven north of Amarillo. You will use the cover of being there to inspect a bull we're interested in purchasing."

The carbonated liquid went down the wrong way, and Francois coughed. His eyes watered as he struggled to catch his breath. Feeling Kellan tap his back lightly, he offered the second a grateful smile.

When Francois finally caught his breath, he rasped, "What do I know about bulls, except how to make zem taste delicious?"

And why would zat call for champagne?

"I said cover, didn't I?" Master Dante smirked.

"Cover for what?" Francois took a sip of his drink just to get some moisture for his throat. Unease filled him, and he shifted in his seat. "What could possibly be so important zat I have to go to some strange coven?"

"How about meeting your mate?" Jared asked, smug amusement in his tone. "Would you go to a strange coven to meet him?"

"These are vampires, handsome." Carson squeezed Jared's shoulder before correcting, "They call their other half a be-loved."

"Ah, yes. My mistake." Jared slid his hand up Carson's thigh as he rumbled huskily, "You gonna give me a refresher on paranormal terms when we get to our hotel room later, In-jun?"

Carson growled softly, his dark eyes narrowing. "I think I should."

Francois watched in shock as Carson sealed his mouth over Jared's. The human openly groped the wolf shifter's dick through his jeans. Carson responded by deepening the kiss and feeding the man a growl.

Feeling arousal sizzle through him at the display, Francois rubbed the back of his neck. His throat felt dry, so he took a deep drink of his champagne. Francois met Dante's smirking visage over the rim of his glass.

"I've already put in a call to Master Jaymes Martinez," Dante stated, lifting his own glass to his lips. "Congratulations, Francois."

My beloved? I'll meet my beloved in Texas?

Stanton, once again attempting to remove his hold, pulled Francois from his memory. Smiling at his confused beloved, he rubbed his thumb over the pulse point at the inside of Stanton's wrist and told his human, "I caused it, so I should fix it."

He didn't mention that, as a vampire, his saliva would heal the wound. Besides, there was no way Francois was going to miss out on tasting Stanton. He'd been wandering the haunted hay maze every evening since he'd arrived five days before — except Tuesday, which had been the prior day, be-cause that was the day the ranch's entertainment was closed. It had been a long, long day.

Finally, the chill on his pant leg caused Francois to glance down. He grimaced upon seeing the large wet and muddy patch on his designer blue jeans. The splotch extended from near his hip to below his knee . . . and he just knew it would stain on the pale fabric.

Unable to help himself, Francois gave in to his need to clean up . . . at least, a little. He released Stanton and pulled the dark-green handkerchief from his neck, using the fabric to swipe at his jeans and flick off some of the mud. Francois had tied the kerchief around his neck to bring out the green in his hazel eyes, and he knew he would have to throw it away later.

No way am I going to tie it around my neck again, even after it's washed.

"Well, uh, sorry again," Stanton stated, taking a step backward. "Um, if I ruined your jeans, I can buy you new ones."

Francois snapped his focus back to Stanton.

Perfect opportunity.

"Okay. What's your phone number, Stanton?" Francois asked as he palmed his phone in his free hand. After a still-blushing Stanton rattled off his number, Francois hit the call button. He heard a chime coming from Stanton's pocket, so he hung up. "Zere. Now you have my number, too."

"Uh, okay." Stanton pulled out his phone and looked at the screen before shoving it back into his pocket. "Well, have fun in the maze." Then Stanton turned and began heading back the way he'd come.

Oh, hell, no!

Francois shoved his phone in one pocket while carefully folding the dirty cloth. As he hurried to catch up with Stanton, he shoved the fabric into his back pocket. He grimaced as he moved, hating the feel of the wet, dirty fabric sliding over his skin.

Ignore it. Ignore it.

After chanting that to himself a couple of times, Francois touched Stanton's wrist as he fell into step beside him. "I will not be calling you to ask for new jeans, Stanton," he told him.

"Really?" Stanton glanced down at him, his scent betraying

his confusion, even over the hint of arousal that had been teasing Francois's senses. "Then why?"

"To ask you on a date, Stanton," Francois replied, recalling that honesty was always the best policy when attempting to woo a human beloved.

Stanton barked a laugh, the skin around his brown eyes twinkling.

Francois lifted one brow, doing his best to ignore the spike of annoyance created by Stanton's response.

After a few seconds, Stanton's laughter ceased. "Seriously?"

"*Oui.*" Seeing Stanton's frown, Francois amended, "It means *yes.*"

CHAPTER THREE

Stanton recognized the look on the slender man's face. He'd seen it on Jerome's face a time or too when Stanton had missed the joke. It was a mixture of exasperation and amusement.

"Oh, uh —" Stanton cocked his head. "Why?" Before Francois could answer, he waved his hands between them. "I mean . . . you're a, what? A fancy French dude, and I work with bricks. Why would you bother?" Then he furrowed his brows and cocked his head. "Or is this a type thing? You got a thing for big guys?"

Francois's expression turned . . . predatory was the only way Stanton could describe it. "Oh, Stanton. Not a type," he all but purred, rubbing his hand up his jacket-covered sleeve. "I have enjoyed both men and women over zee years. You" — Francois pressed closer as he teased his fingertips up Stanton's neck, making the hair on his nape stand on end —"are somezing special, I believe." Scraping his nails along Stanton's neck tendons, he added, "I would like zee chance to find out."

Stanton stood stock still, clenching and unclenching his hands. Arousal burned in his gut, and his blood heated, threatening to give him a raging boner. Only his confusion at why some hot French guy was coming onto him kept him from sporting a throbbing erection.

That would be uncomfortable while walking through a hay maze.

Right. Hay maze. My friends.

"Uh, I don't know." Stanton took a step backward, pulling from Francois's hold. He immediately missed the feel of the man's long, slender fingers on his skin. They'd been soft and sort of soothing. Clearing his throat in discomfort, Stanton rubbed where Francois had been touching him. "I've never done anything with a guy before. Not that you're not hot and all. I'm flattered. Really, but—"

Seeing the way Francois's hazel eyes narrowed, as if annoyed at not getting his way, another thought pushed into Stanton's head.

Maybe he's just playing with me. A vacation romp? I'm nothing special. Why is he pushing so hard?

Stanton sighed. While he'd been telling the truth about being flattered, he had considered doing stuff with a guy before. He'd even talked to Max about it once. Stanton just didn't want his first experience to be with some random stranger.

Or would that be better?

Shaking his head, Stanton decided he would think about it later.

"Sorry again," Stanton repeated himself, peering up and down the aisle, trying to remember where else his friends would have turned. "Have fun in the maze."

"May I walk wiz you, Stanton?" Francois asked, shoving his hands into his pockets and tipping his head to the side. "I have been through zis maze a few times. Perhaps I can help."

"You've been here before?" That caught Stanton's attention. He waved at the hay alley before him and the branch that went to the right. "I think I came down that one, and I turned left and bumped into you. Are you familiar with this section?"

As Stanton spoke, he started forward. He'd already tried to holler for Jerome, but the hay had a surprisingly dampening effect. Plus, there was the noises from the scary decorations.

"*Oui,*" Francois replied, touching his arm before taking the lead. "Zere are three quick splits, so it is easy to get separated or turned around. Zis way."

Stanton followed, surprised to find his gaze straying to Francois's jeans-covered ass. The globes were high and round and muscular. He found his fingers twitching with the desire to cup them, to feel them move under his palms as Francois walked.

Huh. Never felt that desire before.

Taking his next step at an angle, Stanton used the move to adjust his thickening prick.

Perhaps noticing the odd step, Francois peered over at him. His gaze flicked down to Stanton's fly. A small smile curved his lips as he met Stanton's gaze again before licking his lips.

Swallowing hard, Stanton felt his breath catch at Francois's hungry look.

To Stanton's surprise, Francois just winked before pointing to the right. "Let's try zis branch." Then he lifted a brow and asked, "Unless you have been down zere before?"

Yanking his focus back to where it should be—finding his friends—was surprisingly tough.

After clearing his throat, Stanton glanced around again. "Uh—" He frowned as he sighed. "I-I really don't know." Rubbing his palm over his closely shorn head in agitation, Stanton admitted, "Everything is kinda looking the same to me."

"Zat is part of the hay maze's allure. Make most things similar so patrons get turned around." Francois patted his shoulder. "It makes it more fun, because you get lost."

Stanton nodded, figuring the guy was right. "It *is* a maze."

"*Exactemo*," Francois replied, his eyes twinkling in the fake torchlight.

Huh. They're kinda pretty.

"Come, my handsome friend." Francois touched Stanton's lower back, drawing him out of his stray thought. "We will explore zee twists and turns and perchance stumble upon your friends."

Nodding absently, Stanton gave in to the smaller man's

urging and started walking.

Stanton found himself leading for the most part, with Francois staying a step to his right. He had tried to allow him to go first, that way he would have an easier time seeing the motion-activated hay maze scares, since he was so much bigger than him. Except, Francois didn't startle the way Stanton did at the lunging mummies, cackling clowns, or roaring werewolves.

"You don't scare easy, huh?" Stanton commented as they rounded another corner. A witch cackled from her position on a broom as she swooped across the hay maze aisle. Instinctively ducking, Stanton raised his arms over his head as he barked, "Shit!"

As the witch disappeared through an opening between hay bales, Stanton noticed the wire she was attached to. He chuckled softly at his response as he straightened. Standing six-foot-five, he'd felt the wire was a little too close for comfort . . . even though the witch hadn't truly come anywhere close to him.

The designers of the place had, so far, done an amazing job with their motion sensor placement. The scares' noises and movements did the startling while never getting close to the customers.

"You okay?"

Feeling Francois's touch to his lower back, Stanton drew his attention away from where he had been staring at the hay wall. He cleared his throat as he nodded. "Yeah." Pointing absently at the wire—nearly hidden in the evening gloom—Stanton told him, "Just admiring how things were created."

"Hmmm," Francois mused, glancing upward. "Zey did do a fantastic job." Then they started on again, although Francois didn't remove his hand right away. "And in response to your earlier question, it's not zat I don't scare easy. It's zat I've been through zis maze several times already."

Stanton felt the man's fingertips teasing lightly up and down the knobs of his lower spine. The butterflies bounced in his belly for a new reason. His prick began to thicken again, and Stanton almost stepped away from him . . . but he didn't want to be rude.

Yeah, right. That's the reason.

Ignoring the taunting voice in his head, Stanton glanced at Francois out of the corner of his eye. "Then why come back in?"

"To meet you."

Frowning, Stanton cocked his head. "To meet me?" Then his belly twisted for a new reason, and he grumbled, "So, you come into the maze every night to meet a dude to take a tumble with while on your vacation?" Stanton scowled at Francois, and he finally pulled away from him. "I'm not like that."

Am I?

The desire to explore Francois's lithe body certainly made Stanton's fingers tingle with anticipation.

"*Zut,*" Francois muttered under his breath. His brows were furrowed as he grabbed Stanton's wrist, stopping him from moving farther away. "Zat is not what I meant. Do not put words in my mouth, my beloved."

"Put words in your mouth?" Stanton crossed his arms over his chest, pulling free of his grip. "What the hell does that mean?" Feeling his cheeks heat when he realized he'd admitted his ignorance to a hot stranger, he turned and started walking again. "Never mind."

Francois moved so fast, Stanton nearly ran into him . . . again. One second he was behind him, then the next, the handsome guy stood in his path. Upon seeing Francois's flushed cheeks and narrow-eyed expression, Stanton felt a fissure of unease slither down his spine.

Then Francois's nostrils flared, and his eyes widened. Even the blood seemed to drain from his face, leaving him pale in the flickering faux torchlight. Francois sighed as he lifted his palms in a way that encouraged most people to relax.

"We keep having misunderstandings," Francois murmured, the words barely loud enough to be heard over the sound of the witch cackling as people coming up behind them activated the device. After glancing that way, Francois returned his focus to Stanton, evidently dismissing them. "I do not enter zee maze each night to find a lover." He rested his hands on Stanton's chest, rubbing lightly. "I said I was looking for you, Stanton."

Stanton stared uncertainly at Francois. The man's palms on his chest felt firm and warm, even through the fabric of his jacket and t-shirt. Tingles erupted on his skin, and his nipples beaded.

Seeing movement to his right, Stanton took a few precious seconds to glance that way. It gave him time to think of something else. He spotted a pair, a girl and boy, probably teenagers on a date. The girl was dressed in the guy's football pants and jersey, while the boy had a cheerleader skirt on over his jeans and carried pom-poms.

His brain stalling, Stanton stared.

The guy must have noticed, for he rolled his eyes as he passed and muttered, "Discount if we dress in costume."

Stanton nodded. "Oh. Right. Yeah."

While the girl tittered, her gaze glancing between Stanton and Francois—who still had his hands on Stanton's chest—the boy rolled his eyes. With his arm around her waist, they turned a corner and disappeared from view.

Francois lifted one hand from Stanton's chest, only to palm his jaw. His hand was warm and felt smooth against his five o'clock shadow. He used the hold to turn Stanton's head, urging him to return his focus to him.

"I heard you were going to be coming to zee maze, but I did not know zee date," Francois told him as he rubbed his thumb along his jawline. "I was here, wandering zee maze, for a couple of days looking for you specifically, Stanton." Then he lowered his hand to his neck and massaged the tendons lightly. "I am sorry my words upset you."

"Oh." Stanton fought back a shudder as he dipped his head and pressed into the gentle touch. "Mmmm, that's nice."

"Good," Francois purred, continuing to work Stanton's muscles as he skimmed his other hand up a little and rubbed his thumb over Stanton's puckered nipple. "I like zee expression on your face, Stanton. I—"

"Hey, there you are, Stanton."

The sound of Max's tenor yanked Stanton back to the present. He whipped his head around just as the witch's cackle filled the air and her form flew across the aisle. Lilibeth squealed and hid behind Jerome, who'd tensed and ducked.

"H-Hi, guys." Stanton cleared his throat, then swallowed. Nerves fired through his veins, but he couldn't force himself to step back from Francois. "I took a wrong turn."

Jerome glanced between them, his left brow arching inquisitively. "Yeah, so did we."

Lilibeth laughed as she nodded while eyeing Francois. "We found ourselves stuck in a section with one dead end after another and finally figured out how to circle back. We didn't mean to lose you, but we couldn't figure out which turn you took. Although"—grinning, she smirked at him—"it looks like you're just fine. Who's your friend?"

Stanton found his mouth had gone dry, and he was having a hard time getting his throat to work.

Why am I disappointed to see my friends?

Fortunately, Rhyme saved him. "Oh, hey, Francois," he greeted, stopping next to them. "Did you finally find what you've been looking for?"

Francois chuckled huskily as he took a step back, removing his hands from Stanton. "*Oui*, I have."

CHAPTER FOUR

R elief filled Francois when Enforcer Rhyme greeted him, then slung his arm around Max's waist.

Gods be praised, my beloved has friends in zee paranormal world.

That would make drawing Stanton into his world so much easier.

Now, if I can just get him to relax around me . . . and we need to work on zee misunderstandings.

"Join us, Francois," Rhyme encouraged, waving toward the path before them. Then the big vampire smirked. "Just don't show us the quickest way out. These guys are having fun getting lost."

Lilibeth snickered. "You just like the way Max clings to you every time something jumps out and scares him."

"Oh, hush, you," Max snapped back, whapping her upper arm with the back of his hand.

Rhyme drew Max away, guiding them forward. "How could I not love it," he purred as he dipped his head and pecked a swift kiss to Max's lips. "Any excuse to touch you."

Francois thought the same thing about Stanton. He'd quickly recognized that the man would stare at the attractions and become distracted. He figured that was how Stanton had ended up separated from his friends.

But I love how a touch to his back gets him to focus back on me. I'll definitely use zat to my advantage.

"I'm Jerome," a lanky dark-skinned male said, holding out his hand. "Jerome Harsnen. I'm Stanton's roommate."

Francois took Jerome's hand, feeling the man's firm hold.

Resisting the urge to outdo him, he shook and released as swiftly as possible. If this man was Stanton's roommate, he didn't want to get in a pissing contest with him.

"Francois Toulouse. Nice to meet you," he stated.

Jerome opened his mouth, obviously intending to respond, but Lilibeth beat him to it. The vivacious brunette bounced forward and gripped his upper arm. "Hi, I'm Lilibeth, and I love your accent."

Francois allowed her to start them walking behind Rhyme and Max, but he took a second to dip his chin in greeting to the two older humans who were hanging back a little. From their scents, he guessed them to be brothers. He figured he would hear their names eventually.

"Do you still live in France? What part?" Lilibeth continued with her myriad of questions. "Do you love baguettes? Are you in the states for long?"

"Why do you ask another question before he can even answer the first one?" Jerome teased, tugging on the braid her hair was in.

Lilibeth stuck out her tongue, then returned her focus to Francois and beamed at him.

Francois chuckled softly at their playful bantering, noting that nothing in their scents spoke of actual annoyance. He figured the group had been friends for some time to be so comfortable with each other. Thinking of his coven in Montana, he tried to figure out if he had anyone he was that close to.

He couldn't think of anyone. When he'd moved to Master Dante's coven, he had buried himself in work. He hadn't wanted a repeat of what had driven him out of France.

Having no desire to allow his mind to take a trip down memory lane — *zat was a long time ago, and zis is neizer zee time nor place* — Francois shifted Lilibeth's hand on his arm to a more comfortable position. "I spent many years in Nice." That had been his birth coven, and he enjoyed recalling those years. It was the third coven he'd been part of in France that had forced him to leave the country. "It is a lovely place, but I moved to Montana many years ago. I am zee chef at a cattle ranch out zere, similar to zis one, but wizout zee guests." Francois would have preferred to be sharing this information with Stanton, but he figured getting in good with his beloved's friends could only help. "I am here on vacation for anozer couple of weeks."

Technically, Francois had permission to be there as long as it took to woo his beloved . . . but he couldn't tell her that.

Gods, I hope my kitchen will still be in one piece when I get home.

"Wow, tell me about Nice. What's it like over there?" Lilibeth's excitement bled through her tone. "Why did you decide to leave? Was it for your job?"

"*Oui*, for my job." That had been part of it, anyway. "As for Nice—"

Telling Lilibeth about his old home allowed him to focus half his attention on Stanton, who was walking directly behind them next to Jerome. He did his best to control his jealousy. The lithe black man had said they were roommates, and he hadn't smelled of deceit.

Besides, Stanton had already told him that he'd never before done anything with a guy.

Zat doesn't mean Jerome doesn't want to.

Upon hearing Stanton whisper, "What does it mean to put words in someone else's mouth?" Francois lifted his brows.

His beloved didn't recognize the expression?

"Mmm, that means you heard someone say something and jumped to a conclusion about what the person meant," Jerome replied softly, his words slow as if he struggled with how to explain. "Then you say something about what the speaker said, about what he *meant* by his comment, even though you're just making a guess which could be wrong." Then Jerome asked, "Why do you ask, buddy?"

"Earlier, Francois said he was wandering the maze for a

couple of days because he was looking for me," Stanton replied, obviously being honest. "I got upset because I thought he meant he wandered the maze every night looking for someone *like* me that he could take to his bed for a one-night stand. He said that's not what he meant."

"Francois asked you for a one-night stand?" Jerome immediately jumped on that.

Lilibeth squeezing his arm drew Francois's attention, and he realized he hadn't responded to whatever she had said. When he offered her an apologetic smile, she smirked and leaned closer.

"Like Stanton a lot, do you?" Lilibeth winked. "That's certainly how it looked when we walked up."

"*Oui.*" Francois didn't see any reason to deny it. "He is . . . someone who could be very special to me."

Peering behind them with a discreet, side-eyed look, Lilibeth hummed. "Well." She grinned at Francois again. "If the way he's checking out your tight rear-end is any indicator, he's into you, too."

Francois felt a rush of pleasure at that.

My beloved is checking me out. Good.

"We're going on the hayride through the haunted forest once we're done with the maze," Lilibeth told him, a twinkle in her eyes. "You should come."

"I would love to." Since the seer's information had indicated he would meet his beloved in the haunted hay maze, he hadn't checked out anything else.

Lilibeth patted Francois's hand again, then released him . . . just in time to be freaked out by a shrieking ghost. Instead of grabbing him, however, Lilibeth hopped backward a step and once again latched onto Jerome.

Francois smirked as he saw the mischief in Lilibeth's dark eyes, and he realized he had an ally.

Zank zee fates.

They spent another hour wandering the maze. Francois had to bite back a smile every time the humans startled, shrieked, jumped, or ducked. The group didn't temper their reactions, at all, telling how relaxed they were with each other.

During their explorations, Francois stuck close to Stanton. He noticed each time his beloved became lost in admiring the displays and made certain to touch his back before Jerome could. Evidently, the roommate knew of Stanton's quirk, too.

Not surprising, since zey live together.

Francois's actions earned him smiles from Stanton but narrow-eyed stares from Jerome. Since he didn't scent any arousal from the wiry black man, he likened it more to a big brother's protectiveness. Francois would have to figure out a way to win the man over . . . especially if he planned to convince Stanton to move to Montana with him. Fortunately, Lilibeth did a fantastic job of keeping Jerome occupied.

The thought of asking to switch covens so he could stay entered his mind, but Master Jaymes's coven already had a chef and didn't need another.

"You sure you don't want to cozy up to a guy with a little more experience?" a husky voice asked into Francois's ear.

Francois turned his head and spotted Vernon at his shoulder. Beyond him, he could just see Lloyde rolling his eyes. The pair had been introduced as the owners of the company the other humans worked for, but they acted more like goofy cousins — family.

Snorting upon seeing Vernon's teasing eyebrow waggle, Francois shook his head. "I am sorry, Vernon." He swept his gaze over the dirty-blond-haired man, acknowledging that he was a ruggedly handsome fellow. "But you just do not do it for me." Francois shrugged. "Can't change who we are attracted to, can we?"

Vernon rested his hand over his heart and sighed dramatically. "Story of my life."

"Stop being an ass." Lloyde popped Vernon upside the head. "Don't go poaching on the SOs of our employees."

Laughing and rubbing the back of his head, Vernon shrugged. "Not his SO, yet, Lloyde."

"Ignore him," Lloyde encouraged. "Seeing how sexed-up and happy Max is with his man, Vernon is after his own love of his life." Patting Vernon on the shoulder, he shook his head. "Gotta be patient, bro. The love bug will bite you when you least expect it."

Vernon rolled his eyes before grumbling under his breath, "I just wanna get laid."

Francois barked a laugh, quickly lifting his hands to hide his mouth. His mirth drew Stanton out of his conversation with Max about how life-like the vicious bats had appeared to be. It made Francois wonder if Stanton had ever actually seen a bat up close, but it was sort of sweet, none-the-less.

Maybe I will find him a bat to hold.

Smiling at the idea, Francois watched as Stanton crossed back to him. He had never held a filthy bat in his life, but for his beloved . . .

Odd thought.

"What's going on?" Stanton glanced between them. When Lloyde rolled his eyes and shook his head, Stanton frowned. "What?"

"Vernon made a pass at me," Francois stated, seeing no point in not telling the truth. Reaching out, he didn't resist his impulse to grab Stanton's hand and twine their fingers. "I am certain it was in jest, but even if he was serious, you are zee one I want."

Stanton's eyebrows furrowed as he shifted his gaze to their hands. "I don't understand why. I'm not anything special."

Francois shrugged. "And neizer am I." Then he tugged and began heading down the path again. "Come. I believe we are nearing zee exit."

Even as Stanton heaved a deep sigh and muttered, "Good.

I gotta piss," he didn't break contact with Francois.

He took that as a win.

CHAPTER FIVE

Stanton couldn't believe how annoyed he was that his boss had hit on Francois. Hadn't it been obvious that the hot French guy was into him? Shouldn't that have made him off-limits to flirt with?

I'll have to ask Jerome when I get him alone.

That ended up being sooner than Stanton had expected. After they exited the maze, they checked the time for the next ride through the haunted forest. They had just over thirty minutes.

While everyone else headed off to get treats from the food vendors, he and Jerome got in the line for the port-a-potties. As they waited, Stanton voiced his confused frustration.

"Vernon hit on Francois, and I'm pissed about it. Why?" Stanton crossed his arms and frowned at the ground as he continued on a whisper, "And why would Vernon even do that? It was pretty obvious when you walked up that he's into me. Right?"

Then Stanton lifted his chin and met Jerome's gaze, curious how his friend would respond. His buddy had always helped him sort his thoughts. To his surprise, Stanton found Jerome's black eyes wide and his lips slightly parted.

Stanton realized he'd shocked him.

Huh. Why?

Jerome snapped his mouth shut, then opened it again. He cleared his throat and glanced around. Finally, Jerome must have found his tongue.

"Uh, that means you like him," Jerome muttered, his gaze

flicking from Stanton to the ground and back again. "As in . . . *like* like him. You're attracted to him, and you want to explore that, and you don't like the idea of competition and someone else taking him away from you."

Stanton nodded, agreeing with everything Jerome had said. He made it sound so simple. Still, he struggled with the concept.

"I've never liked a dude enough to do anything with 'em before," Stanton admitted. "Have you?"

Jerome coughed into his fist, then jerked his chin down in a tight nod. "Yeah, man. I have." He pointed at the line of johns. "Your turn, Stanton."

Turning, Stanton noticed the slightly ajar door of an empty stall ten feet away. He nodded and headed inside. Making quick work of using the facility, he relieved his bladder with a sigh.

Once Stanton had finished, he exited and went to the hand-washing station. Jerome met him there.

"So what should I do?" Stanton asked, resuming their conversation. "Francois wants to take me to his bed, but he's only here for a couple of weeks." He'd overheard the man's comment to Lilibeth. "Is it better to learn from someone you're never gonna see again? Or should I look for someone to date?"

Stanton felt his gut twist a little at that idea. His attraction to Francois was strong . . . really strong. Would he be able to find another guy that he *like* liked so much?

Jerome sighed heavily as they fell into step and headed toward the food vendors. "This is one of those things where . . . I can give you advice, but you're the one who ultimately has to make the decision." He paused and gripped Stanton's shoulder, giving it a brotherly squeeze. His expression held a serious quality that Stanton rarely saw on his relaxed friend's face. "You have to decide because *you* are the one who has to live with the consequences."

Stanton nodded, understanding. "Okay. So what's your advice?"

The corners of Jerome's lips twitched. He held Stanton's gaze for a few more seconds, and then he glanced around the space. Stepping closer, he tipped his head up so he could whisper into Stanton's ear.

"If you're gonna learn about man-sex, then you want a partner who's patient and giving. See if he'll suck your cock."

Gaping, Stanton jerked backward. He stared at Jerome as shock filled him. "Really?"

Jerome chuckled as he nodded. "Sure. If he wants you in his bed so bad, he needs to earn the honor."

Stanton cocked his head. "Honor?"

"Absolutely." Jerome pushed at his shoulder, then started forward again. "I know you don't hook up much, so maybe you'd like to get to know someone before doing the horizontal tango." His brows furrowed as he peered at Stanton. "If that's your bag, you could make him take you out on a date."

Furrowing his brows, Stanton sorted through Jerome's words. Sometimes, his buddy began talking in slang, and he had to ask for clarification. He figured *horizontal tango* was clearly sex, but why was Jerome talking about his bag? Bag of what?

"My bag?" Stanton voiced the question, trusting Jerome to explain.

Jerome grimaced. "Sorry, man." He pointed, indicating that they were coming up on a table where their friends were sitting, eating, and waiting for them. "Saying if that's your bag is another way of saying if that's what you prefer."

"Okay. Weird," Stanton muttered under his breath. "Who comes up with this shit?"

When Jerome just laughed and shrugged, Stanton figured the man didn't actually know.

Falling silent, Stanton made his way to the table. He spotted the empty chair beside Francois and headed toward it. To his delight, he saw a plate before the seat, and it contained his favorite treat—fried bread covered in powdered sugar as well as strawberries and whipped cream.

"Oh, wow," Stanton rumbled, settling on the chair. "Is this for me?" It seemed pretty obvious, due to the placement, but he didn't want to steal someone else's dessert.

"It is." Francois held out a fork. "Lilibeth said it is your favorite?"

Stanton took the fork as he nodded and grinned. "Yeah, it is. Thanks." After stabbing the tines into the edge of the fried bread, he flashed a wide smile Francois's way. "Thank you. This was awful nice of you."

"It is my pleasure," Francois replied, his voice turning husky. "My only request is will you allow me to try a bite?"

"Oh, yeah." Stanton cut off a piece of the crispy, sugary goodness, then slid it through the strawberry sauce. He finished by stabbing a strawberry piece and swiping up a small dollop of whipped cream. "Here." Lifting the fork toward Francois's face, Stanton offered, "You should have the first bite."

Instead of taking the fork, Francois opened his mouth and leaned closer.

Stanton eased the forkful of food into Francois's mouth even as he felt his cheeks heat. Seeing the slender, refined-looking man's lips wrap around the tines, he swallowed hard. His gut clenched, and his mouth watered . . . and not in anticipation of the food.

Instead, an image that shocked Stanton pushed into his mind—taking those lips in a deep, plundering kiss . . . so he could taste the sweet concoction from the other man's mouth.

Sucking in a sharp gasp, Stanton tore his focus away from Francois's heated expression. As he prepared a piece of the treat for himself, he inhaled deeply. He tried to regain control of his breathing, which suddenly felt too fast.

Stanton took a bite. To his relief, the flavor of the sweet, strawberry goodness burst across his tongue, driving all thought from his head. He hummed appreciatively and chewed quickly as he cut off another bite.

While shoving his second forkful into his mouth, Stanton heard Francois chuckled roughly. "If you make zose noises every time you eat zat, Stanton, I will buy it for you daily."

His cheeks began to heat again when he chanced a glance Francois's way.

Clearing his throat, Stanton mumbled, "Can't eat this kinda thing every day. Would get fat."

"Zen I would just have to find a way to help you work it off."

Stanton gaped at Francois, his hand stalling halfway to his mouth. He took in the self-satisfied smirk curving the pale man's thin lips as well as the twinkle in his hazel eyes, more green than brown in their gleam. The look on Francois's face once again pulled Stanton's attention to his lips . . . or maybe that was the dab of chocolate at the corner of his mouth, a left-over remnant from the chocolate ice cream cone he'd been eating.

The sound of his strawberry plopping off his fork yanked Stanton's attention away from Francois.

"You and Francois can gaze heatedly at each other later, Stanton," Rhyme teased, tapping his shoulder. "The ride leaves in ten. Eat up."

Focusing on his food, Stanton grunted.

As Stanton chewed, Francois leaned toward him and whispered, "I'm not sorry I distract you so, Stanton." He rested his hand on Stanton's thigh and squeezed. "You do zee same to me."

Stanton glanced Francois's way again. Even with the heat

gleaming in the man's eyes, his focus again slid to the choco-late on his mouth. After swallowing, Stanton gave in to temp-tation.

Reaching out his free hand, Stanton gripped Francois's neck. "I don't understand why I'm so attracted to you," he muttered as he leaned closer. Then he swiped his tongue along the corner of Francois's mouth, cleaning him of the chocolate.

"I will explain it to you in time," Francois murmured, his chest rising and falling quickly, telling Stanton how affected he was by his move.

"Okay." Then Stanton pecked a light kiss to Francois's lips and pulled away.

Francois swayed toward him before catching himself. His tongue flicked out, and he licked his lower lip. "You are a tease, Stanton."

Shaking his head, Stanton smiled at him. "Naw." He pointed his fork first at his dessert. "You bought me this epic dessert, and it would be rude of me to waste it." Then he waved it in a circle, indicating the area. "And we're in the middle of a seating area that's filled with families. This isn't the place for the kind of kisses I wanna lay on ya."

Stanton's face heated when he shared his admission, but it was the truth. He wanted to really taste the man. He'd never experienced such a deep desire.

But should I ask for that blowjob or not? Stanton shoved his food into his mouth, although he was barely tasting it now. *Would asking for a date make me come off as a prude, since he's only in town for a short stay?*

His gut churned for a second at the thought of Francois leaving. He had to swallow hard to keep his treat down. Shak-ing his head at his tumbling thoughts, he used the last of the bread to wipe up any remaining traces of strawberry sauce and whipped cream.

"All right, then." Rhyme stood, and Max bounced out of

his seat. "Let's throw away our trash and get to the ride. I already texted Tyler. He's the one loading people, so he knows to save us seats." The guy waggled his eyebrows. "Being friends with the employees has its perks. Otherwise, we would have needed to get in line at least fifteen minutes ago. This thing always fills up fast." Wrapping his arm around Max's waist, Rhyme picked up his and his partner's stack of dirty paper plates and napkins with the other. "Come on."

Damn, that is nice.

Everyone followed Rhyme's example.

As they strolled over to the staging area for the start of the hayride through the haunted forest, Vernon fell into step beside Stanton.

Stanton just kept his frown off his face.

Vernon must have read something in his expression, however, for he twisted his lips into a wry smile. "Sorry about hitting on your man, Stanton." He bumped his shoulder into Stanton's, adding, "I didn't realize you were meeting a date here. It won't happen again."

Sighing, Stanton admitted, "I met Francois in the maze. He isn't my date." Then he felt Francois squeeze his opposite hand where he walked on his other side, and he realized he needed to amend that. "Uh, I mean, I guess he is now, um, sort of." Stanton furrowed his brows as he glanced Francois's way. "Is this a date?"

Francois's eyes twinkled in the evening light as he lifted their twined fingers. "Even if you do not consider zis a date, Stanton, I would love to take you out." He nipped at Stanton's knuckle, the bite stinging lightly even as a tingle went up Stanton's arm. "It would be my honor to be seen around town wiz you."

Stanton sort of felt the opposite. Francois was suave and confident, lean and pretty with his toned frame and aristocratic features. Stanton would be honored to be seen dating this man.

Guess that answers that, too.

Turning back to Vernon, Stanton stated, "Apology accepted." Then he frowned as a rush of possessiveness flooded his gut. "Don't do it again."

Vernon laughed as he nodded. "You got it."

Grinning happily, Stanton helped his *date* onto the hay wagon.

Chapter Six

Keeping his hands mostly to himself on the hayride was one of the hardest things Francois had ever needed to do in his life. Now that Stanton had begun to accept his advances — and in part, their connection — he wanted to get him alone so he could move them forward as swiftly as possible. The scent of the man's blood filled his nostrils, causing his mouth to water.

The small drop Francois had helped himself to from Stanton's knuckle when he'd kissed it in no way satisfied him. Due to knowing he would be meeting his beloved, he hadn't taken a donor for over a week. Instead, Francois had been living off bagged blood.

I am so ready to end that habit.

Drinking bagged blood just wasn't the same as enjoying the succulent life-giving fluid from the source. On top of that, he knew sustenance from his beloved would be better than anything he'd ever experienced. Even just the couple of drops he'd had over the evening caused his pulse to race and sent energy zinging through him.

Instead, Francois settled for occasionally massaging Stanton's impressive thigh muscle. After all, there were children on the ride. It helped that Rhyme kept offering him encouraging looks.

Francois didn't know much about the vampire, but he thought that was nice of him.

On the ride, Francois found he enjoyed watching Stanton's enthusiasm. The huge human seemed to have an inner light that burst out whenever he grinned or shouted enthusiastically. Stanton's voice was so deep and rough, but his brown eyes appeared to glow with his happiness any time he pointed at some new, interesting display set up in the woods.

Stanton laughed when he saw the set-up of the mad scientist electrocuting the man. His human winced when they trundled past a display of a man being drawn and quartered. At least the limbs were still attached. Although the recorded screams and cackling of the other men were threatening to send chills up Francois's spine. When they saw an animatronic Baba Yaga scooping stew out of her big black pot — which was full of fingers and toes — cries of, "Eeewww," erupted from those on the ride, Stanton and Francois included.

Between displays, there were plenty of ghosts, flickering lights, shrunken heads, and more hanging from branches.

Francois found himself impressed.

That didn't mean he wasn't grateful when the almost hour-long ride came to an end.

After everyone had unloaded, Vernon and Lloyde said they were going to call it a night. They headed toward the road, opting to walk the dimly lit path instead of waiting for the wagon. Lilibeth had grabbed Max's hand, and they'd darted toward a booth that sold tickets for the games. Rhyme immediately followed.

"What about you guys?" Jerome asked, glancing between them. "You going to check out the games?"

Francois lifted one brow as he smiled up at Stanton. "What would you like to do, handsome?" Winking, he asked, "Would you like me to win you a stuffed dog?" Francois pointed toward the game where you threw a dart at a balloon.

For a second, Stanton's brows furrowed. Then a crooked smile spread over his lips. "Only if you let me win you a goldfish."

Stanton indicated the booth where he needed to land a ping-pong ball into one of the small, water-filled jars that had a goldfish in it. There were dozens of jars, and only a handful had fish in them. The table also rotated.

"You zink you can do zat?"

Francois found himself impressed at just the idea. While he could throw a dart with deadly accuracy, he couldn't toss a ball for shit. He had learned to chuck knives over a century before after his coven had been invaded by a pack of wolf shifters bent on taking over their coven's land. They'd been rogues who'd banded together and didn't have any territory of their own. Their coven grounds had been located on the outskirts of Nice and would have afforded the rogues plenty of space to run in wolf form.

He'd ended up locking himself in the pantry when three shifters had converged on him at once. One or even two — maybe — he could have handled. Once he'd been saved by the enforcers and trackers, he'd decided to learn how to give himself a ranged weapon — his knives.

"Yeah, I can do it," Stanton replied confidently. "I used to pitch in softball."

While Francois didn't know how that correlated, he nodded anyway. "Let's go get some tickets, zen."

"I'll join ya'll," Jerome fell into step with them. "Give your ticket to Max or Lilibeth. They're already almost to the front of the line."

"That's cutting," Stanton countered, shaking his head and heading toward the end.

Jerome laughed, grabbing his arm and stopping him. "No, it isn't, Stan. It would only be cutting if you got in front of them in the line." Jerome began guiding him toward the front of the line. "There's still the same number of transactions because all you're doing is giving them your ticket to exchange for more game coupons."

Stanton nodded with furrowed brows. "Okay."

Francois cocked his head, trying to figure out why Jerome had spoken to Stanton that way. It didn't seem to be one friend giving another crap. Then Francois remembered how Stanton had asked Jerome to explain putting words in another's mouth.

Huh. What's up with my beloved?

Knowing he wouldn't figure it out while standing off to the side, he quickly hustled forward as he pulled out his wallet. He gave Max some money and made his request. Max nodded as he leaned close.

"Is he your beloved?" Max whispered into his ear.

Francois would have thought Rhyme had already told him that Stanton was. Maybe the human just wanted to confirm. Unable and unwilling to deny what Stanton was to him, Francois nodded once.

Max nodded back, his brows furrowing. "Be good to him." Then he moved to the ticket counter.

Once everyone had their tickets, they meandered through the games. Francois stopped at the dart-throwing booth and handed over his tickets, and the human behind the counter gave him three darts. After hefting each one, he easily used them to pop three balloons.

"What color stuffed dog would you like, handsome?" Francois asked, just managing to taper his smile so he wasn't showing off his fangs.

"Uh, blue."

The attendant handed over a blue medium-sized stuffed dog.

They moved to another booth, where Max tried to toss a ring onto bottles. It took him buying rings three times, but he finally managed it. He then gave the teddy bear to Rhyme.

Francois had needed to cover his mouth with his hand to hide his amused smile.

They reached the ping-pong ball toss, and Francois found

himself doubly impressed. It took all three balls, but Stanton sank one into a jar with a goldfish in it. When a grinning Stanton handed him the plastic bag holding the fish, Francois wondered what the hell he was going to do with it.

Guess a trip to town to get supplies is in order.

At the next booth, Rhyme zinged the baseball at the milk bottles, easily knocking them from the pedestal. He gave the stuffed cat to a little girl who'd been passing by . . . who was dressed in a cat Halloween costume. After confirming that Francois didn't mind, Stanton gave the dog to her slightly older sister, who was dressed as a fairy. Their brother received the bear.

A moment later, they noticed a clearly disappointed pair of young ladies at the booth they'd just left. One woman held the hand of the second, assuring her that it didn't matter if she won or not. Then she gave the clearly disappointed girl a kiss.

Francois glanced at Stanton and held up the bag he carried. Stanton huffed softly as he smiled. Crossing to the pair, he waited until they stopped kissing lightly before clearing his throat.

Both women turned to face him. The blonde muscular woman glanced at him, then beyond him, and obviously noticed the group of buff guys behind him. She stepped forward and half inserted herself in front of the smaller, plump brunette that she'd been trying to win a fish for.

Ignoring the unspoken insult—as if Francois would hurt the lovely ladies—because he knew others would if they thought they could get away with it, Francois offered her a soft smile as he held up his bag holding the goldfish. "Sometimes, it is not how you play zee game, but what happens after." Using his thumb, he pointed over his shoulder at Stanton. "My partner won zis for me. I zink it would mean more to zee two of you."

The blonde's jaw sagged open. Her eyes widened in obvious shock, and she glanced from him to whomever over his shoulder and back again. It was the brunette who slipped around the blonde and smiled shyly up at him.

"That is so very sweet of you, but we couldn't possibly take your fish," she said as she twined her fingers with her lady friend's. "Your partner won it for you. It wouldn't be right."

"Naw, you take it." Stanton slung his arm around Francois's shoulders, tucking him against his huge broad body. "It was just us guys doing that whole one-upping each other thing." The friendly handsome guy winked as he added, "Besides, I already gave away the stuffed animal that Francois won for me. It's only fair."

"I—" the brunette started, glancing between them. Her gaze lingered longingly on the fish.

"Thank you." The blonde had recovered, and she reached out and took the goldfish bag from Francois's hand. Holding it up for the brunette to look at, she lowered her voice. "I told you Fate would provide."

"Fate?" The word was out of Francois's mouth before he could help himself. He took a quick, discreet sniff, confirming that the pair were human. "You believe in Fate?"

"Oh, yes," the brunette stated confidently. She pressed her shoulder against the blonde's as she peered at the fish, using the index finger of her free hand to rub against the side of the plastic bag. "My mother knew my father was provided by Fate when he spent every dollar he had just so he could win her the beta fish she wanted." A blush crept into her cheeks as she beamed lovingly at her partner. "It's not a beta, but I couldn't resist wanting one when I saw them being offered as a prize."

Francois nodded, understanding. "I, too, believe in Fate." He sent a side-eyed look Stanton's way as he added, "Knew zis man was mine zee second I tasted him."

The blonde snickered as she batted her eyelashes at him. "Oh, kinky."

Stanton tensed next to him, and his cheeks turned a dark shade of pink. "Not like that."

Both women laughed. Then they started with their thanks. "You guys are too kind." The blonde turned and smiled at the woman whose hand she held. "Are you ready to go get this guy some fresh water?"

"Mmm-hmm." The brunette nodded eagerly.

"Bye!" the blonde called as the brunette waved, taking the bag and tucking it against her breast protectively.

Francois began to lift his hand, intending to say his good-bye, too. Then his gut tightened, and a fissure of unease trickled up his spine. Acting on instinct, he started after them.

While Stanton glanced at him in confusion, he fell into step beside him.

"Hey, I know zee guy driving zee tractor. I will make certain you get a seat." Francois waved a hand, seeing their rebuttal coming a mile away. "Zee path is dark, after all. You don't want to trip and hurt zee fish."

After exchanging a glance, the pair shrugged and nodded.

"Thanks," they said almost in unison.

Francois knew he'd made the right decision when, just before they reached the field where the tractor turned around and stopped to pick up passengers for the return trip, a pair of men Francois didn't know stepped from behind some trees.

"Aww, you don't wanna go with them," the dark-haired man stated with a sneer. "They wouldn't know how to treat you."

"We told you we're not interested," the blonde replied belligerently. "Now, get out of the way."

"I don't think so," the guy said. "And I have the friends to prove it."

Another three men appeared from amidst the trees, and the brunette clutched the fish's bag even tighter as fear permeated her scent.

Well, shit.

CHAPTER SEVEN

"Anthony, Benjamin, what are you doing?" Stanton frowned as he glanced from his co-workers to the three men he didn't recognize. Seeing the mix of leers and sneers, he fought back a shiver. He didn't like the way a couple of the guys were looking at the ladies they'd given the fish to.

"Walk away now, Stanton, and we'll leave you alone." A smirk curved Benjamin's lips, giving his Hispanic features a nasty glow. "Call it . . . a co-worker courtesy."

"Why do you want the ladies?" Stanton asked, easing closer to the women. "They planned to go home."

Anthony stalked forward as the other men began to close in. "Their night has just had a change of plans." He began reaching for the blonde, but she glared at him and batted his hand away. "You shouldna done that, pretty."

"Don't you fucking touch me," the blonde snapped.

Laughing, Anthony declared, "I'm gonna do plenty more than touch you."

"No, you will not," Francois countered. "People like you make me sick. Men who zink zey are macho but cannot take no for an answer." His eyes were narrowed, and he sneered at them. "You are nuzzing but a bully."

Stanton figured Francois was really angry because his French accent had thickened. The slender man's body even seemed to be vibrating. His hands were clenched into fists, and he looked like he was about to launch himself at Anthony.

Snorting, Anthony swept his gaze up and down Francois's

lean frame. "What are you gonna do about it, faggot? In your designer jeans and name brand jacket." Curling his lip, he rested his gaze on the muddy splotch that had dried on Francois's thigh. "You let our big dummy get you dirty, ass-licker? You like a little dirty romp in the hay?" Anthony cupped his crotch and gave it a blatant squeeze. "After we're done with the ladies, maybe I'll let you blow me."

A rush of protectiveness the likes Stanton had never felt swelled inside him. He grabbed Francois's shoulder and surged forward, putting himself between Anthony and everyone else. Pointing at Anthony, he growled, "You're an asshole, and I won't let you touch any of them."

Benjamin stepped closer, muttering, "Come on, Stanton. Don't make waves. They ain't worth it." Shaking his head, he added, "Can't see why you're even hangin' with all those queers."

Stanton glanced at Anthony, who looked like he was getting ready to take a swing at him, and Stanton shifted his feet, wanting to be ready. He'd been in his fair share of scraps, although he'd always had Jerome to back him up. Absently, he wondered how long it would be before his friend came looking.

"No, Benjamin." Anthony cracked his knuckles. "Stanny-boy here made his choice."

Just as Stanton had anticipated, Anthony swung. Instead of trying to dodge, he lunged closer. His co-worker's punch landed on his upper arm with little power, but Stanton's gut jab caused the other man to stumble backward.

Stanton heard a commotion behind him, and movement to his left drew his attention. To his surprise, Rhyme held one of the strangers' arms behind his back. He glanced around and noticed the others were detained as well. The other strangers were held by a pair of workers dressed as vampires — one male and one female. Benjamin, on the other hand, was lying face-down on the ground, and Francois gripped one of his wrists, pressing it to his upper back, while his knee was resting at the small of Benjamin's back.

"Wow. Francois?" Stanton heard the amazement in his own voice.

Francois smiled at him, the expression tight. "He tried to hit you when you were knocking Anthony back."

When Francois curled his lip into a sneer and turned his head to peer down at Benjamin, Stanton thought his canine looked really sharp.

Must have been because of the shadows.

"How does it feel to be taken down by a faggot?" Francois taunted. "Not a good idea to make assumptions, hmm?"

Stanton wouldn't have thought the man could fight.

Go figure.

Turning, Stanton peered around. "Where's Anthony?" Meeting Rhyme's gaze, he added, "How'd you know we were in trouble?"

"I texted zem while zey were taunting us," Francois told him. His brows furrowed in annoyance. "And zee asshole ran away when he saw his buddies were caught."

"Shit," Stanton grumbled, crossing his arms over his chest. "I shoulda grabbed him." Then he remembered who else they'd been protecting and spun around. He spotted the blonde holding the brunette, who still held the bagged fish. "Uh, pardon my cussin'."

His momma would roll over in her grave for his behavior. She'd always reprimanded their father when he swore in front of her. Of course, that didn't stop the man from—

Stanton shoved those thoughts away when the blonde laughed. Rolling her eyes, she quipped, "I'm pretty sure Cindy's mouth is way worse than yours . . . anytime the umpire makes a call against the Yankees."

The brunette, Cindy's cheeks darkened a bit. "I'm not that bad."

"Yes, you are," her girlfriend countered. Then she pecked a kiss to Cindy's lips. She lifted her head, then held out her hand to Stanton. "I'm Amanda, by the way."

"Nice to meet you," Stanton said as he shook her hand carefully. "Sorry about my asshole co-workers." He glared at Benjamin, wishing he'd had the foresight to stop Anthony from fleeing. "Please tell me you're pressing charges."

Amanda and Cindy exchanged a look. "Well," Cindy began slowly. "They didn't really do anything to us except make threats." Her brows furrowed. "Do we really have anything to pin on them?"

"Oh, hell yeah," Rhyme stated gruffly. He obviously didn't have a problem with swearing in front of women. "These assholes were stopped from attempting assault and rape. We're gonna pin plenty of shit on them."

"Hey, we didn't touch 'em," the guy in Rhyme's arms cried as he began to struggle.

"But you had intended to." A broad-shouldered, dark-haired man strode into the clearing. His dark eyes glimmered with anger from under the brim of his cowboy had as he peered at the man who'd spoken. "And that is what is important."

Then the malevolence from his expression cleared, and Stanton finally placed him—Jaymes Martinez, the owner of the ranch. He focused on the blonde. "My deepest apologies that something like this happened on my ranch." He held out his hand. "I'm Jaymes Martinez. Please know that I have people looking for Anthony, and he will *not* leave this ranch a free man."

"Oh, um, thank you," Cindy replied, taking Jaymes's hand and shaking.

Amanda shook next, saying, "It's not your fault. Assholes like that just kinda crawl out of the woodwork at the most unexpected times."

Jaymes rested his hands on his hips as he eyed the men being held. "Indeed, they do." A cold smile curving his lips, he stated, "Murdoch, if you would take Benjamin off Francois's hands, my people will take these assholes somewhere where they can cool their heels while we wait for the police."

A lean, toned guy that Stanton recognized as a wrangler who handled trail rides approached Francois. After Benjamin traded hands, the four employees began frog-marching the attackers through the woods. Before disappearing, Rhyme called, "Max and Lilibeth are with Jerome at the ring toss game. Will you let him know I'll be a few minutes?"

Stanton nodded. "Yeah."

"Can I offer you ladies a free meal while we wait for the authorities?" Master Jaymes asked, guiding the women back toward the festivities. "I'm afraid they'll have a few questions."

"Like when Anthony and Benjamin hassled you the first time," Stanton commented, remembering Anthony's opening remarks.

"Hmmm, yes. I would like to hear what was said," Jaymes rumbled, a soft growl in his voice.

Francois gripped Stanton's hand and tugged, gaining his attention. "What about you, Stanton," he asked, sweeping his gaze over his torso. "Anzony hit you. Are you okay?"

Stanton squeezed Francois's hand, surprised to see so much concern in his eyes. His chest squeezed a little. He found he liked that expression.

"Eh, I'm fine," Stanton assured, not wanting to worry the other man. Grinning, he winked. "Anthony telegraphs his movements, and he punches like a girl."

"I would still like to check you for injuries," Francois pressed, his expression earnest. "You stepped in front of me, tried to protect me. I am flattered." Then he smirked as he gave him a heated gaze. "Alzough, it was unnecessary."

Nodding, Stanton murmured, "I didn't see you take Benjamin down, but he's a pretty thickly muscled guy. He hangs drywall for the company I work at." Then he frowned as a thought struck him "Huh. He'll probably lose his job now though. Him and Anthony. They got in trouble not long ago and were on probation." Rubbing the back of his neck, Stanton mused, "Even though this happened outside of work, I figure Vernon and Lloyde will still sack 'em."

Francois growled softly. "It is zee least zey deserve." Then he touched Stanton's hand again. "And I would still like to make certain you are okay."

"Oh, sure." Stanton unzipped his jacket, revealing his navy-blue t-shirt. After tossing his jacket over his shoulder, he pointed at his left bicep. "That's where he hit me. No mark." Stanton rubbed over his muscle, flexing experimentally. "Doesn't even hurt."

A soft moan drew Stanton's attention back to Francois. The other man's focus was riveted to his pectorals, and he glanced down, realizing when he'd tightened his bicep, he'd flexed them as well. He began to feel an embarrassed heat wash through him, but upon hearing the way Francois cleared his throat and seeing his tongue flick out to swipe over his bottom lip, that heat morphed into a different kind. Stanton realized that Francois liked what he was seeing.

That open appreciation caused the same reaction that it had every time he'd seen it that evening. His prick plumped in his jeans, and his nipples beaded, aching to be touched. He shifted his weight restlessly as he grabbed his jacket from his shoulder and tugged it on.

"Mmmm, no wonder you want to get him alone," Amanda teased. "I may be a big ol' lesbo, but even I can see your man is a hunka maleness."

Francois smirked at the ladies. "Zat he is." He turned back to Stanton. "And I believe I will need to inspect more zan just your arm."

Resting his hands on Stanton's torso, Francois used his thumbs to flick his still-beaded nipples. Even through the fabric of the jacket, it still caused a zing to shoot through him, and he sucked in a harsh gasp. He gaped, and his brows shot up at Francois's brazen move.

Right. He called me his partner earlier. Is this normal partner behavior?

"Uh, w-well—" Stanton stuttered as he glanced around uncertainly. "I should really tell Max about Rhyme. Then maybe we could, uh—" After looking around again, Stanton finished, "Not sure where we could go, though."

"I know where to go," Francois assured, sliding his right hand down his stomach to his hip. He squeezed before releasing him. "Let's go find Max." With his left hand, Francois again took one of Stanton's.

When Stanton glanced around, he spotted a smiling Cindy giving him a discreet thumbs up. Then she turned and followed Jaymes with Amanda's arm around her waist. Jaymes, however, wasn't nearly as subtle.

Peering over his shoulder at Francois, Jaymes stated, "Be certain no one is around, Francois. This is a family show."

"I will, Master Jaymes," Francois replied, dipping his head in acknowledgement of what had clearly been an order. "I have explored zee area fully over zee last couple of days."

Jaymes chuckled as he nodded and led the ladies away.

Stanton felt heat rise in his cheeks. Somehow he just knew they all thought they were going somewhere so Francois could inspect him for more than just injuries.

Why would they think that?

CHAPTER EIGHT

Francois kept his palm on Stanton's lower back as they offered a quick explanation to Max, Lilibeth, and Jerome. Once done, he claimed they were going to take a minute to step away and make certain they wouldn't have anything more than bumps and bruises from the encounter. Then they would have to give their statements to the cops before leaving.

"Did you want me to come with you?" Jerome offered, focusing on Stanton. He pointed. "I think I saw the first aid station in that direction."

"Zat is unnecessary," Francois countered . . . too quickly, judging by the narrowing of Jerome's eyes. Thinking swiftly, he added, "Anzony is still on zee loose. I zink Rhyme would prefer you stay wiz Max and Lilibeth."

"Uh huh," Jerome muttered, crossing his arms over his chest as he leaned against the side of the booth. "Well, we'll be here for a bit, probably." His expression turned teasing as he glanced from Lilibeth to the ring toss game. "Lilibeth is" — he cleared his throat on a snicker — "having trouble."

"Oh, shut it, you," Lilibeth snapped, bumping his hip good-naturedly. "It's not always about winning. I'm having fun."

"If you say so," Max commented with a laugh.

"We'll see you in a bit," Francois assured, then applied gentle pressure to Stanton's back to get him moving. "Let's go."

Francois felt the hairs on his nape stand on end as he

moved away from the trio, and he just knew if he glanced behind him, he would see Jerome watching them.

Overprotective big brother type. Huh.

While Francois wondered what caused that reaction, he was happy to wait until later to ask.

I am finally getting my beloved alone.

"Come zis way," Francois urged. He removed his hand from Stanton's back so he could grab his hand. Twining their fingers, he squeezed as he tugged lightly. "I was exploring zee other day and found a quiet place nearby."

"Um. Okay."

While Stanton sounded uncertain, he didn't resist. Francois counted that as a win. The shadows lengthened as they passed the last couple of hanging lanterns. Having been planning to meet his beloved, Francois was prepared. He pulled a small flashlight from his jacket pocket and flicked it on.

"Were you a *Boy Scout* when you were young?"

Francois chuckled as he shook his head. "No, my beloved Stanton." He winked as he added, "Grew up in France. No *Boy Scouts of America* over zere. I like to plan ahead."

"Always a good policy," Stanton commented. "Jerome says something similar about carrying condoms."

"Oh?" While Francois had no desire to hear about Stanton's past conquests, he couldn't help but ask, "What does Jerome say about carrying condoms?"

Stanton chuckled under his breath. "It's better to have it and not need it, then need it and not have it."

Francois joined in as he nodded. Once he spotted the big rock near the crooked tree he'd been looking for, he veered toward them. "Zis way."

After ducking under a tree branch, Francois turned sharply and slipped between some brush. He lifted several bushy pine limbs and held them, so Stanton could step past him. Hearing his human's surprised gasp, he grinned but tempered the expression before releasing the branches and joining him.

The stream that flowed along the edge of the small clearing glittered in the moonlight. A span of ten-by-twenty grass made a soft place to rest. The tall trees, the deep brush, and the remote area offered them a high level of privacy.

On top of that, Francois's superior vampire hearing would allow him to hear anyone coming . . . even over the trickle of the brook.

"This is pretty beautiful," Stanton commented, sweeping his gaze around the area. "The moonlight filtering through the tree drapes everything in shades of gray, which is even better than the light of your flashlight."

Francois was happy with that idea. Clicking off his light, he shoved it back into his pocket. Then he stepped up beside Stanton.

To Francois's surprise, Stanton sported an expression of wonder on his face. His big beloved smiled serenely, and his gaze slowly panned over everything. He shoved his hands into his pockets, and the tension was gone from his shoulders.

Then Francois recalled how often Stanton had focused on the design of the displays.

"You're an artist," Francois mused softly. "But I thought you worked in construction."

Stanton jerked his focus back to Francois. His smile turned wry as he lifted one shoulder in a half-shrug. "Jerome calls me an artist. I'm a bricklayer, so I guess he's sorta right. I design walkways and retaining walls and fit stones together to make them look nice with the landscape." Stanton's eyes took on a vacant expression as he murmured, "Like, there was this one mosaic design that a customer wanted, and I—" Pausing, Stanton cleared his throat. "Aww, you don't wanna hear about that shit." His brows furrowing, Stanton glanced around the space before focusing on Francois. "This place is kinda romantic, so . . . um . . . what did you have in mind?"

Francois rested his palms on Stanton's torso and slid them

beneath the open jacket's flaps. Enjoying the hard flesh beneath the soft fabric of the worn blue shirt, he slid his hands up and pushed the jacket sideways. Stanton seemed to understand the silent demand, for he shrugged out of it, allowing it to drop to the grass.

"I wanted to check you over for injuries," Stanton reminded his sexy beloved. "Wiz my hands and tongue."

"Y-You do?" Stanton's chest rose and fell swiftly as he stared down at Francois. "W-Will you, um, suck me?" His cheeks took on a slight pinkish hue even as he added, "'Cause your touch is making me hard."

"Mmm-hmmm," Francois purred, scraping his nails back down Stanton's chest, flicking over his nipples in the process. "I would be delighted to drink your seed."

Stanton groaned roughly, his body vibrating beneath Francois's touch. "Wh-What do you want me to do?"

Francois inwardly grinned, pleased to discover Stanton's submissive nature. Tugging on the hem of his human's shirt, he insisted, "Take zis off, zen lie on zee grass."

The swiftness of Stanton's obedience caused Francois's own shaft to twitch. The earthy fragrance of his beloved's arousal caused an answering burn in his own veins. As he watched Stanton spread his shirt and jacket on the ground, then lie upon them on his back, he adjusted his hard dick behind his fly.

While Francois would much rather have opened his pants to relieve the pressure on his erection, he didn't know how Stanton would respond to that . . . since he was inexperienced with being intimate with a man.

And I am zee one who will change zat.

Kneeling, Francois swung one leg over Stanton's hips. The crotch of his jeans hugged his balls from him having to spread his legs so wide. Between that sensation and seeing Stanton sprawled under him, Francois moaned with delight.

"Gorgeous, my big beloved," Francois crooned. He would

forever deny the tremble in his hands as he lowered them. When his palms landed on Stanton's huge pectorals, his breath came out in a gasp. "Oh, Stanton," Francois crooned as he began tracing his human's thickly muscled torso. "You are a treasure, beloved."

"Wh-Why are you c-calling me b-beloved," Stanton stuttered, obviously just as affected by Francois's touch as Francois was to be touching him. "Y-You like pet names?"

Francois lifted his gaze to Stanton's flushed face, pleased to see his lips parted on panting breaths. His eyes were dilated, and a sheen of sweat made his forehead gleam. When Stanton slipped his tongue out and wet his lower lip, Francois let out another moan.

Need to feel that under his own crashed through Francois.

"Francois?"

Upon hearing Stanton's uncertain whisper of his name, Francois struggled to focus. He slid his hands up so he could draw his face closer to the other man's. "It is not just a pet name, Stanton. I will explain in time." Dipping his head, Francois nuzzled his smooth cheek against Stanton's. The rasp of his human's five o'clock shadow caused tingles to erupt on his neck and shoulders. "I wish to kiss you now, Stanton. May I?"

"Uh, I . . . yeah."

Then Stanton brought his hands up and gripped Francois's jaw. He gave in to his human's press, allowing him to guide his face to Stanton's own. For an instant, Stanton held him there, staring into Francois's eyes.

Francois slid his right hand up and scraped his fingernails across his scalp. "Relax, Stanton," he urged. "Let me make you feel good."

Stanton nodded, his hold easing.

Taking that as permission, Francois sealed his lips over Stanton's. He licked lightly along the plump lower flesh, learning his human's skin's flavor. His nip to that skin gave Francois what he wanted. Stanton gasped, and Francois slipped his tongue inside.

Francois moaned softly as he lapped along Stanton's teeth. Sliding his tongue against his beloved's own, he reveled in the flavor of sweet sugar and lingering strawberry from his dessert treat. Beneath that was something unique, a masculine buttery taste that had to be all Stanton's own.

Delicious!

Feeling Stanton's tongue teasing along his fang, Francois groaned. A shudder worked through his body, and hunger caused his gut to clench. Even his erection twitched and leaked in his jeans.

Jerking up, Francois broke the kiss and stared, panting, down at his human. His human sported a loopy smile and met his gaze. He licked his lip in what probably wasn't meant in a provocative way, but it yanked a moan from Francois anyway.

Stanton chuckled as he grinned up at him. "You taste good." Then his brows furrowed. "You have fangs like those guys dressed as Dracula. Why?"

"I'll explain later," Francois promised. Then he waggled his eyebrows. "But first, I must check you all over."

Without waiting for an answer, and needing to distract Stanton, Francois dipped his head again. He began kissing and lapping down one line of Stanton's jaw, then up the other side. He worked the skin under his ears, then down the column of his neck, pausing to suckle on his Adam's apple.

Stanton grunted and arched his neck, giving Francois more room.

Francois sucked harder, licking and nipping the bobbing bump of flesh.

"Sh-Shit," Stanton whined, gripping Francois's upper arms. "Y-You're gonna mark me."

"Would zat be so bad?" Francois asked between licks to the

bump.

Groaning, Stanton shook his head.

Francois thought that meant Stanton didn't want him to continue, so he began working the rest of the way down his beloved's neck. Reaching the flesh where his human's neck met his shoulder, he paused to work the area, longing to sink his fangs in and drink deeply. His mouth watered, and he quickly moved on for fear of giving in to his desire.

As Francois began mapping Stanton's pectorals with his lips, teeth, and tongue, he used his hands to tease along his beloved's ribcage and abdominals. He relished the way his human grunted, groaned, and twitched beneath him. Ignoring the possibility of grass stains on the knees of his jeans, Francois slowly knee-walked backward as he made his way down Stanton's torso.

When Francois's fingers encountered Stanton's jeans, he lifted his head. "May I open your jeans, Stanton?"

"God, yes," Stanton rumbled, his voice husky and deep with a hint of a needy whine. "I want your mouth on me so fucking bad."

Pleased beyond measure that he had reduced Stanton to such desire, he opened his human's jeans.

Francois moaned with delight upon seeing what Stanton was packing. He also thanked the gods that he was a paranormal. His beloved's erection was perfectly proportioned with the rest of him—namely, huge. Trying to get his human's thick, at least ten-inch cock up his ass would take some prepping.

Note to self, buy some butt plugs.

Seeing the bead of pre-cum bubble up from Stanton's wide slit and with the heady scent of his human's thick arousal teasing his nostrils, Francois didn't bother with more teasing.

Francois opened his mouth and wrapped his lips around Stanton's wide, flared head. He swept his tongue over his crown. When his man's flavor hit his taste buds, Francois

moaned with delight.
    Delicious.

CHAPTER NINE

Stanton groaned roughly as he peered down at Francois. The sight of his lips stretched around his swollen crown, the feel of them, caused his gut to clench. He already felt the telltale tingle at the base of his spine after all the teasing Francois had done to his body. His balls felt heavy and full, and only clenching his hands in his shirt kept him in check enough to keep from thrusting.

"O-Oh fuck!" Stanton whined, doing everything in his power to maintain control. "I-I'm close already. H-Holy shit, your mouth." He felt his hips twitch despite himself, and through gritted teeth, he warned, "P-Pull off. Gotta thrust. D-Don't wanna h-hurt you."

On more than one occasion, upon seeing Stanton's size, his hook-up would give him a tug instead of sucking him.

That was why it didn't surprise Stanton when Francois took him up on his offer and popped off his dick. Lightly stroking his erection, using his spit for slick, Francois met his gaze. Then he grinned and winked, opened his mouth, and sank back down on him.

Stanton didn't even have time to comment on the fangs in the man's mouth. Instead, he barked a cry as he felt exquisite suction all the way to his root. To his shock, the slender, out-of-his-league Frenchman buried his nose in Stanton's pubes, lodged his crown in his throat, and swallowed around him. A second later, Francois sucked strongly as he pulled partway off again . . . only to sink back down.

After only two more repetitions, Stanton couldn't stay still any longer. He planted his feet and bucked. Panting harshly, groans and grunts rumbling from his throat, he jabbed up once, twice. Then his balls pulled tight, and before he could offer a warning, Stanton poured his seed down the other man's throat.

Stanton's head swam, black spots dancing across his vision, and he groaned Francois's name. Panting harshly, he whimpered as he felt the other man continue to suckle on him. When his softening dick grew sensitive, he whined and shifted restlessly.

Francois lifted, allowing Stanton's penis to slip from his lips. Rubbing the back of his hand across his wet lips, he growled softly as he swept a satisfied gaze over him. He rose to his knees, revealing that he'd opened his pants.

Sucking in a surprised gasp upon viewing Francois's long slender erection, Stanton felt his fingers twitch. He watched as the other man began jacking himself, the movement of his fingers damn near mesmerizing. All the while, Francois peered down at him with a feral gaze.

Even his eyes seemed to have an odd red light in them.

Unable to remain still, even as sated as he felt, Stanton reached up. He batted Francois's hand away from his prick. Francois's brows shot up, and his erection bobbed. Stanton didn't leave him hanging.

Stanton wrapped his fingers around Francois's erection. Slowly, he slid his fingers up and down, learning the feel of the warm rigid flesh. It felt silky smooth beneath his fingers, and for a second, he worried his callouses would bother Francois.

Then Francois groaned and rocked into his touch.

Taking that as confirmation of his enjoyment, Stanton picked up his speed. The angle was a little odd, him being below the erection he touched, but he still found it fascinating. He teased his fingertips over Francois's crown, rubbing in the pre-cum gleaming there, then massaged the wrinkled skin beneath his flared head before stroking him again.

Francois groaned. "Harder," he pleaded, shuddering above him. He flexed and released his fingers, obviously struggling with what to do with them. "Please!"

Realizing he'd essentially been teasing, he tightened his grip.

Moaning, Francois sped up his ruts. After two more, he fell forward, resting his hands on Stanton's shoulders. He gripped tightly as he bucked, fucking Stanton's fist in sharp jerks.

Stanton reached under Francois with his other hand and gripped the man's balls.

Gasping Stanton's name, Francois froze.

Grinning up at Francois, Stanton squeezed lightly, then rolled the orbs within their silky sack. At the same time, he tugged on Francois's shaft.

Francois's jaw sagged open, and his eyes seemed to roll back. His ecstasy at Stanton's ministrations were on clear display. In the next instant, Francois shuddered hard, and Stanton felt the wet spray of his release coat his abdominals.

Stanton felt a bubble of smug satisfaction fill him. His gaze on Francois's teeth, he grinned. "Didn't realize you'd dressed up as a vampire, too, Francois." His sluggish brain to mouth filter seemed to have turned off after Francois's awesome sucking abilities. "You gonna bite me with those things?" As Stanton spoke the teasing words, he tilted his head to the side in invitation.

Francois's eyes snapped back open . . . and the irises were blood red.

Gasping, Stanton froze.

Then Francois lowered his head, hiding the red from view as he licked a swipe up his neck. "May I, Stanton?" he hissed softly. "Would you like another orgasm?"

"Yes." The word was out of Stanton's orgasm-mushed brain before he could think better of it. "Y-You really wanna bite me?"

Francois licked up his neck again, lingering to suckle on his pulse point. "Yes, I would love to bite you, and you will love my bite."

Stanton felt a fissure of fear surge through him.

What the fuck?

"Easy, Stanton," Francois rumbled, sucking on his pulse point. "You are safe. Always safe wiz me."

To Stanton's surprise, feeling Francois's mouth on him and how he'd started to stroke over the skin of his ribcage, his concern ebbed to be replaced by a fresh wave of arousal. It suddenly occurred to him that he'd never had back to back orgasms before. Could he take the risk?

His arousal surging south, causing his prick to thicken anew, did the thinking for him.

"God, yeah," Stanton mumbled, arching his neck further. "Don't know what you're doing, but please don't stop."

"I am pleasuring the other half of my soul."

Stanton's eyes widened, but then he felt sharp teeth sink into his skin. A spike of pain caused him to suck in a harsh gasp. A second later, that was followed by the sweetest, tingling sensation he'd ever experienced.

The tingles trickled down his chest, causing his nipples to bead. His gut clenched when the sensation hit his abdominals. Upon feeling it slither down his treasure trail, he bucked under Francois's grip . . . which turned out to be surprisingly strong.

Then it hit him.

Francois was sucking on his neck, and each pull of his lips sent more and more of those tingles throughout his body. When they finally hit his groin, his balls pulled tight.

Groaning roughly, shivers racking him, Stanton arched as his orgasm surged through him. His eyes rolled to the back of his head as waves of heady bliss pinged through his body. He couldn't help the hisses and groans or even the jolts racking him.

Stanton didn't know how long he floated. He finally came back to himself to the ring of a cell phone and the feel of Francois petting his chest. Grunting, he peeled open eyelids that he didn't remember closing.

"*Oui*, Master Jaymes. My beloved sleeps. I will — Ah, wait. He has just woken." Francois smiled at him from where he reclined on the grass beside him, resting his weight on one elbow. He used his other hand to hold his phone to his ear, even as he held Stanton's gaze. "No, I have not explained, but I am certain Max and Rhyme will help. We will be to speak wiz zee police as swiftly as possible."

After that, Francois hung up. He set his phone aside as his lips curved into a tentative-looking smile. "My beloved," he purred. "You asked what zat meant . . . and now you know." Returning his hand back to Stanton's chest, Francois began skimming his fingertip over and around his nipple. "I am a vampire, and you are zee ozer half of my soul. I have searched for you for centuries." Francois's mouth curved into a smile, which was filled with concern. Rubbing his palm up Stanton's chest, he scraped over his scalp soothingly. "I would never hurt you. You're everyzing to me."

Stanton sucked in a slow, harsh breath as he swept his gaze over Francois's face. Licking his lips, he noticed how the man was no longer tempering his expression. That meant as he spoke, the tips of his fangs flashed in and out of view.

"So — " Stanton thought over Francois's unexpected words as swiftly as possible. "Vampires are real." As he watched Francois nod, Stanton recalled his lover's words on the phone. *God, I have a lover. Wait. Do I have a lover? Oh . . . another thing —* "I have a couple of questions."

Francois nodded as he pushed to a sitting position. "Zat is

to be expected." Rising to his feet, he held out his hand. "But now, we must talk to zee police. May I have your word zat you will not share anyzing about vampires wiz zem?"

Stanton scoffed as he placed his hand in Francois's. That noise turned to a bark of surprise when he found himself easily tugged to his feet. Staring down at the much smaller man, he gaped.

His expression earnest, his hand still gripping Stanton's, Francois murmured, "Do I have your word, Stanton?"

Jerking a nod, Stanton stuttered, "Y-Yeah. Yeah." Then he rolled his eyes. "Don't know much anyway, except you bit my neck, and I came like a fucking geyser." Speaking of which, Stanton peered at his torso. "You cleaned me up."

"No man enjoys waking wiz cum crusted in his chest hair." Francois rubbed the palm of his free hand down Stanton's chest, causing his skin to goose bump. "Or on smooth skin that begs to be licked and sucked."

To Stanton's shock, he felt his blood begin to heat once more. "Damn." He grabbed Francois's hand. "Why do you make my blood heat like no one I've ever met?" Cocking his head, he swept his gaze up and down the lithe, sexy man. "Is it because you're a vampire?"

"No, zat is not it. Rhyme is a vampire, too, and you are not attracted to him." Francois pulled his hand from Stanton's grasp as he took a step backward. He pointed down. "Do up your pants, Stanton. Seeing your sexy naked body is making it hard to zink of anyzing but completing our bond."

"Bond?" Stanton shook his head and waved his hand. Then he bent and yanked up his half-off jeans, righting them and doing up his fly. "Okay, stop giving me more fodder for questions. You say I'm your soul mate, and I'm your beloved, and you said something about Rhyme and Max being able to help." Stanton grabbed his shirt off the ground as he continued to ramble, trying to sort his thoughts. "Shit, Rhyme is a vampire, too?" Frowning, he added, "Maybe that's why—" Stanton cut himself off, knowing he needed to focus. Inhaling slowly, he recalled Jerome's advice. Think of one thing at a time. "Vampires. I guess the two important questions are these. How could Rhyme and Max help? And what does it mean that I'm your beloved? Your soul?"

Francis bent and handed Stanton his jacket. After pulling on his t-shirt, he took the jacket. He slipped that on, too.

"First," Francois began. "You will not speak of vampires to anyone but Max and Rhyme . . . until I've had time to explain everyzing fully."

"Fair enough," Stanton agreed, nodding.

Francois inhaled deeply, licked his lips, then stated, "As I said, Rhyme is also a vampire. Max is his beloved, zee same as you are my beloved. A vampire has only one beloved on zee planet at any given time, and when zey meet zat person, zey become zee most important person in zee world to them." Gripping the bottom of Stanton's jacket, Francois slowly zipped it up as he focused an intense look his way. "Zat is you to me, Stanton. You are my soul. My life. My eternity. And I will do anyzing I can to keep you safe, happy, and healzy."

"Oh," Stanton whispered, his mind reeling.

I did ask.

Chapter Ten

Francois tapped his forefinger on the steering wheel. He swallowed hard as he shifted in the seat. His heart raced, and his palms sweated.

Growling under his breath, Francois focused on his breathing. He had known he'd piled too much too fast on Stanton. As soon as he'd allowed his human to see his fangs, the man had begun to question and doubt. That had been clear . . . in hindsight.

Except, after over a week of waiting and dreaming and wondering who his beloved would be, then seeing Stanton take a hit for him, Francois's vampire nature had taken control. He'd needed to care for and please his beloved. He'd needed to confirm that he was well and satisfied.

That had been everything.

Unfortunately, his nature had brought about some uncomfortable questions . . . and they hadn't had time.

After they'd talked to the cops, Stanton had told Francois that he was heading home with Jerome. That his beloved was going home with another totally infuriated him as a vampire, but he'd hidden his possessiveness. Instead, Francois had made certain to remind Stanton that they'd swapped numbers and had extracted a promise that Stanton would text him when he reached home safely.

Stanton had complied, but he'd ignored Francois's calls after that. He hadn't picked up or called him back. Since his beloved had to work, he had tried to be patient.

Unfortunately, since Stanton hadn't replied after two days,

and it was now Friday, Francois had broken down and talked to Rhyme. Good thing the vampire enforcer had been way ahead of him.

Rhyme had been encouraging Max to get closer to Stanton, to make himself available if he wanted to talk. According to Max, Stanton had asked a couple of quiet questions, but in truth, the guy had been damn busy at work. Evidently, a rush job had come in that had Stanton going to a site south of the city by six in the morning—plus, Anthony and Benjamin had lost their jobs, so they were short workers—and he was putting in twelve and fourteen-hour days.

Francois could only imagine how exhausted Stanton would be every evening. His need to care for his beloved had been shoved into overdrive. To Francois's relief, Max had given him Stanton's address.

To appease his vampire's need to care for his beloved, Francois had prepped a large meal. There was enough for Jerome, too, if the man ended up being there. While Stanton would prefer to have his beloved to himself, something told him he needed to stay in the other human's good graces.

Jerome could make convincing Stanton to complete their bond very difficult.

Bonding. Another thing I still haven't had the chance to explain.

Shaking his head, Francois narrowed his eyes as he spotted Rhyme's SUV's brake lights. Max had decided he and Rhyme needed to take him there personally. He appreciated it, since that meant the door couldn't be slammed in his face.

Rhyme was still on the fence about explaining vampires to Jerome, but Francois would if he needed to.

Francois slowed his *Buick* and followed Rhyme's SUV around the turn. Glancing left and right, he took in the condominiums and apartment complexes. While he understood the need for such styles of homes in the city, he cringed at the idea of having to live in one. As a paranormal, he liked his privacy.

Wonder how long it will take to convince Stanton to move to Montana. Another thought struck him. *Huh. Maybe I should invite his buddy, too. Of course, that means explaining vampires to the guy.*

Tipping his head, Francois cracked his neck. He followed as Rhyme turned into the parking lot of a large apartment complex. His tension returned, causing his shoulders to tighten.

"Relax," he hissed at himself.

Inhaling deeply once again, Francois parked his vehicle. He let it out on a long deep breath. By the time he finished one more inhale and exhale, Rhyme was tapping on the window and smirking at him.

Francois opened his door and muttered, "Shut the fuck up. Not all bondings go as smoozly as your own did."

Rhyme snorted. "I took Max out on a few dates before explaining vampires to him." Stepping backward, he shoved his hands in his jeans' pockets as he quirked an eyebrow at him. "You decided to jump in feet first."

Grimacing, Francois nodded. "Yeah. Probably not my finest decision."

"Thinking with your dick can make even an experienced man do that." Rhyme patted him on the shoulder. "Grab the meal, Fran. I'm hungry."

As if on cue, Francois's stomach growled.

Laughing, Rhyme turned away. "Come on, lover boy. Let's get you to your guy."

Francois was more than on board with that. He swiftly rounded his car and pulled open the rear door of the passenger side. After handing a bowl of mixed green salad to Rhyme—who'd followed him—Francois grabbed the pot roast and dumplings. He used his hip to close his vehicle's door, then followed Rhyme up the walk, and then the stairs.

Max already stood at the door. Considering Jerome appeared to be trying to bar him entrance, the little man seemed to be attempting to talk his way inside. When Jerome spotted Rhyme and Francois, his eyes narrowed.

"What's going on here?" Jerome asked gruffly. His dark eyes glittered with irritation. "We didn't have anything planned. We just got off work after a long couple of days, and all we want to do is relax with a pizza and a coupla beers."

"That's why we're here, Jerome." Max sounded almost exasperated. "Because we know you and Stanton had a rough couple a days. Even with that overtime bonus the bosses offered you, surely this has been a tough order to fulfill." He pointed over his shoulder with his thumb. "Francois is a professional chef, and he's brought us an epic meal." Lifting his other hand, Max hefted the bowl he carried in it. "And I have dessert." Grinning and winking, Max added, "I know how much you love my banana vanilla pudding."

Jerome's eyes widened, and his gaze snapped to the bowl. "Banana vanilla pudding?"

Rhyme nodded. "Oh yeah." Wrapping his arm around Max's waist, he pushed closer. "And I have salad, and if you let us into the kitchen, Francois will bake the pot roast and dumpling dish he's carrying." Waving his hand, Rhyme told him, "Now back up. I'm hungry."

Even though he still cast a wary eye in Francois's direction, Jerome backed up. He pointed to the left. "Kitchen is that way."

Francois obeyed the silent order. As he turned and headed in the direction Jerome had indicated, he noticed the sound of a shower running somewhere close by. The image of a wet, naked, soapy Stanton popped into his mind. Francois mentally groaned as his blood rushed south and his body heated with need.

Gritting his teeth, Francois glanced over his shoulder, hoping no one had noticed his untimely boner. He spotted how Jerome turned to Max and gave him a pointed look. Sadness and frustration flooded Francois as he headed to the kitchen . . . too bad it didn't do much to ease his arousal.

Just what the hell did Stanton say about our time together to cause such a change in Jerome?

Francois set down his pot roast platter, then adjusted his erection. Heaving a soft sigh, he eased himself into a more comfortable, and discreet, position. He thought about untucking his shirt, but he figured that would just draw attention to his predicament.

When Stanton had left, he'd seemed to be fairly calm. Jerome had been a little standoffish after hearing about what had transpired with his co-workers, but he'd still been cordial. Perhaps after a couple of days picking up the slack caused by the loss of Anthony and Benjamin, Jerome was just tired and cranky.

Gods, I hope Stanton kept his promise and didn't say something he shouldn't have.

Breaking promises was never a good way to begin a relationship.

No jumping to conclusions. As Francois mentally scolded himself, he turned on the oven to pre-heat. *Focus on the here and now, on taking care of my beloved.*

After that mental pep-talk, Francois turned and . . . nearly rammed into Jerome. He backed a step, finding his lower back pressed against the counter. The man was only a couple of inches taller than him, but he still seemed to loom as he placed the salad bowl on the counter.

After another narrow-eyed frown, Jerome turned and opened his refrigerator. He placed the dessert inside before doing the same to the salad. Jerome closed the door, then returned his focus to Francois.

"I don't know what you did to my best friend, but I won't let you hurt him," Jerome hissed as he leaned close to him. "Even if that means I have to force you out of his life."

Francois licked his lips slowly as he held Jerome's fierce

gaze. He mentally weighed the pros and cons of what he should say. *Paranormals or not, vampires or not . . .*

Finally, Francois decided, "I don't want to fight you for Stanton's affections, Jerome." He lifted his hands in placation. "He is your best friend. I hope we can be friends, too." Upon scenting the mistrust still rolling off Jerome in waves, Francois added, "I do not know why you are upset wiz me. I do not know why Stanton is upset . . . if he is. He has not returned my calls."

As much as Francois hated admitting ignorance, he had to be honest. Maybe he could get some information that way. At least this conversation had caused his erection to die a quick death.

Jerome crossed his arms over his chest as he rocked back on one foot. "Maybe he's just not that into you and doesn't want to hurt your feelings." He smirked as he continued, "He's nice like that."

Francois shook his head, not believing that for an instant. "Stanton and I have enough chemistry to light a fire, Jerome," he claimed smugly. "I am certain he just needs time to come to grips wiz having a relationship wiz a . . . guy."

Jerome stepped closer again and lifted his hand. "You live in Montana. Are you going to rearrange your life for him and move here?"

"I—"

"Jerome, why do you have Francois backed into a corner?"

Stanton's voice drew both men's attention, and Francois sucked in a harsh gasp. "*Zut alors*," he mumbled, cussing under his breath as he drank in the view.

Stanton stood at the opening of the kitchen. His close-cropped hair shown in the light, betraying that it was wet. Wayward beads of moisture gleamed on his bare torso, making Francois's mouth water. The pale jeans he wore hung low on his hips, showing off the deep vee of his hip grooves.

Shifting his weight from foot to foot, Stanton cleared his throat. "You look like you want to eat me," he muttered, his voice gruff. His focus slid to the left as he added, "What are ya'll doing here?"

"Max told us about what a beastly few days you all have had." Rhyme appeared with Max tucked against him. "Francois volunteered to bake you guys a filling meal, and Max brought the banana pudding you both like so much."

"You brought me food?" Stanton sounded a little confused. "Why? I've been ignoring you."

"You have indeed been ignoring me," Francois repeated, saddened to hear that it had been a conscious decision on Stanton's part. "I zink I understand why, however." The beep of the oven, indicating that it had finished pre-heating, drew Francois's attention. "Do you like pot roast, Stanton?"

After opening the oven door, Francois slid the platter inside. He closed the door and leaned against it. Shoving his hands into his pockets, he barely managed to refrain from crossing the room and tracing his fingers across the lines of Stanton's torso.

My beloved is just too damn tempting.

It didn't help that when Francois focused on Stanton's face, his human snapped his gaze back upward. His cheeks took on a pinkish hue, and he shuffled his feet. Then he crossed his arms over his chest.

Hmmm . . . I do believe my beloved was checking out my ass. Nice.

"Uh, yeah. I like pot roast." Licking his lips, Stanton met his gaze once more. "Sorry about ignoring you. I—" He paused, cutting a look Jerome's way. "What we did together. Uh. I needed time to process it."

Francois nodded slowly. "It was a lot to take in." Unable to stay away, he pushed away from the closed oven and started toward him. "Zat is why I kept sending messages, so you would know I was zinking of you and was here when you are ready with questions." Then Francois lifted his hand, palm up. "But staying away from you wizout knowing you are well is difficult."

Stanton stared at Francois's hand for one heartbeat, then two, before reaching out and placing his own upon it.

Relief flooded Francois as he slid his fingers between Stanton's.

CHAPTER ELEVEN

The tension Stanton had been carrying in his shoulders immediately began to ease. He squeezed Francois's hand lightly as he smiled widely at the slender man. Having Francois reach out to him, ask for his touch, caused his heart to thud in his chest.

Why did I refuse to return Francois's calls? The man is — oh, right . . . vampire.

"Okay, what's going on?" Jerome cut into Stanton's confusing thoughts. "You refuse his calls, get all close-lipped about what you two did together, and now you're holding his hand?" Resting his hands on his hips, Jerome sported a concerned expression. "Talk to me, buddy."

Stanton glanced from Jerome to Francois and back again. He opened his mouth, but no words came out. He hadn't talked about his time with Francois because he didn't know how to separate everything. Pretty much, when Jerome had teased him about getting his first blowjob from a guy, Stanton had stuttered a yes, blushed, then muttered about how he didn't want to talk about it.

Jerome had asked him if Francois had hurt him. Stanton had assured his friend that wasn't the case. When Jerome pressed, he'd waved his hand, shook his head, and claimed he just needed time to think.

That was true, too . . . but that didn't change how he noticed Jerome watching him like a hawk.

"Grab beers for everyone, Jerome," Rhyme encouraged, in-

76

terrupting the awkward moment. "While we wait for Francois's amazing meal to cook, we'll sit and explain why Stanton has been having a hard time adjusting." Then Rhyme grinned broadly, showing off his fangs. "It's really not what you think."

Gaping, Jerome stared at him. "What the hell?" Cocking his head and narrowing his eyes, he added, "Do you wear them all the time when it's near Halloween?"

"Not at all," Rhyme said, winking. "These aren't something I wear. My fangs just are . . . because I'm a vampire." Still grinning, he waggled his eyebrows. "Yep. We exist."

"You're about as subtle as a wrecking ball, babe," Max commented dryly.

Stanton snorted, then released Francois, so he could head to the fridge and get the beers Rhyme recommended.

On second thought . . .

Pausing, Stanton opened the cupboard to the left of the stove and grabbed the bottle of whiskey.

Three hours later, Jerome lay snoring in his favorite recliner. After great food and ample amounts of whiskey, the man had accepted the existence of vampires. They'd all sat down to watch a movie, and ten minutes in, his friend had conked right out.

Rhyme and Max chuckled as they rose.

"Where are you going?" Stanton asked from where he sat on the love seat with Francois pressed against his side.

Grinning, Rhyme stated, "You guys want to be doing something other than sitting and watching a movie." He touched his nose, then cast a pointed look at their crotches. "Vampires have an enhanced sense of smell, and you both reek of need. Go fuck and complete your bond."

"Bond?" Stanton recalled hearing that before. "I still don't know what that is."

"I will explain," Francois told him.

Waving, Rhyme and Max headed toward the door. When they reached it, Rhyme opened it while Max turned back toward them. "Got plenty of lube?"

"I . . . uh"—Stanton felt his face begin to burn—"yeah."

He'd bought some the night before because his dick was getting sore from all the jacking off he'd been doing.

Max laughed and gave him a thumbs up. "Have fun, guys."

Then they exited, closing the door behind them.

Stanton nibbled his bottom lip, trying to decide what he was supposed to do. Even if Francois had been a woman, he wouldn't have known how to make his move. At bars, women always pursued him.

"May we go to your bedroom, Stanton?" Francois asked softly, rubbing his thigh with one lean-fingered hand. "I wish to be able to speak freely." His gaze strayed to Jerome for a few seconds before smiling up at him. "And I wish to be alone wiz you."

Nodding, Stanton rose. "I wanna be alone with you, too," he admitted, helping Francois to his feet.

Still holding the vampire's hand—he found he really enjoyed the simple intimate contact—Stanton grabbed the remote. He turned the volume down a little, hoping the rumble of the TV would cover any noises they made. Plus, it should help keep Jerome asleep, especially after all the alcohol his friend had consumed.

Stanton placed the remote on the coffee table, then led the way down the hall to his bedroom. As he opened the door, he felt a wash of embarrassment at the state of his room. The place was sort of a mess, since his long hours had left him exhausted every night when he came home.

Releasing Francois, Stanton began picking up his dirty clothes. He heard the snick of the door's lock as he dropped the jeans and underwear into his laundry basket. When he returned to his room, Stanton found Francois closing the distance between them.

"Relax, Stanton," Francois urged, resting his palm on Stanton's torso. "While I do normally like a tidy room, zat can wait." Then his glance strayed to the unmade bed before he refocused on Stanton and gave him a hungry smile. "Besides, wiz what I hope for, we would be mussing up zat bed soon anyway."

"Oh, yeah?"

"Mmm-hmmm."

Stanton smiled as he rested his hands on the slender man's waist. His hands were so big that he could practically wrap them around him. Knowing he didn't have to temper his strength caused a surge of relief to fill him as he slid his palms under Francois's shirt.

"Last time, you got to explore," Stanton commented as he gripped the hem of Francois's shirt and began to lift it. "Can I explore you today?"

"You may explore me anytime you wish, my beloved," Francois replied, lifting his arms to facilitate Stanton pulling his nice polo shirt over his head. "I am yours and will do whatever you wish to give you pleasure." Then Francois grimaced and added, "As long as it does not put your life in danger."

As Stanton folded the polo shirt in half and draped it over a chair, he nodded his head. "That makes sense." Then he turned back and licked his lips as he admired Francois's pale, toned form. He reached out and skimmed his fingertips over one perky pink nipple, then traced around the light tan areola. "Your body is beautiful, Francois." Lowering his gaze, Stanton followed it with his fingers, teasing over his flat stomach, then down his treasure trail to the button of his designer jeans. "Can I take these off, too?"

Francois nodded, so Stanton began unbuttoning and un-zipping.

"Will you take off your clothes, too?" Francois asked, his voice filling with huskiness. "I would love to see you again." Then he grinned cheekily. "And it would be difficult to complete our bond otherwise."

Stanton opened his mouth to answer as he unzipped Francois's fly, and all thought fled. Spotting the erection he'd been dreaming about touching again, of tasting, Stanton teased his forefinger over the already damp crown. He licked his lips as his mouth watered.

"Oh, beloved," Francois whined, shifting in Stanton's hold. "You need to stop if you don't want me to blow first thing."

Chuckling softly, Stanton admitted, "I'd like to see that." Then he glanced at the bed beyond Francois and growled softly. "Although, I want to taste you even more."

Then Stanton pushed Francois's jeans down his legs. "Tell me about bonding. What is it?" From the word usage, he could guess, but he didn't want to possibly misunderstand something.

Francois lifted his leg at Stanton's urging, explaining as he undressed him. "Bonding is simple, but you need to understand that it can never be undone." Peering down at him, shifting his weight to his other foot so Stanton could remove his shoe, sock, and finally his pant leg, Francois looked at him with a serious expression. "To complete our bond, I will spill in your body while feeding from you." Francois reached down and traced along Stanton's jawline, possessiveness filling his eyes. "Zen, our life forces will be bonded, and we will live togezer, forever."

"Live together?" Stanton asked as he slowly rose to his feet. He began peeling off his clothes and nodding absently. "Yeah, that's what couples do. Max moved in with Rhyme really fast." As he shoved his jeans down his legs, a thought hit him.

"But you live in Montana. Do you expect me to move up there?"

Francois sighed, his features turning troubled. "I hope to convince you to move zere, yes."

Standing naked before an equally nude Francois, Stanton was having trouble concentrating. Still, he knew the conversation was important. He sighed as he rested his hands on his hips . . . just to keep himself from reaching for the other man's delectable body.

"Can you move here?" Stanton asked curiously. "Get a job as a chef around here?"

Wincing, Francois rubbed the back of his neck. He backed up and settled on the side of Stanton's bed, shoving the blanket aside in the process. Resting his hands on his thighs, Francois nodded slowly.

"I could. I would need to petition Master Jaymes, so I could become part of his coven." Francois cocked his head, his eyes going vacant. "Zey already have a chef for zeir ranch, so I would need to find somezing in town to occupy my time while you are working." Then Francois refocused on Stanton and smiled at him. "Unless you would like to quit? I have plenty of money. Zere is no need for you to work."

Stanton stared at Francois, processing what he'd said. The vampire had to change covens in order to stay around there permanently. He was willing to give up his position and change his way of life . . . for him.

Shaking his head, Stanton crossed to the bed. "Naw, don't try to do all that. Me and Jerome, we can move."

Francois's brows shot up. "Please know your best friend is welcome to come," he told him slowly. "I see how he behaves more like a big brozer, but can you really speak for him?"

Now that Stanton had decided on his future, he felt settled. It was similar to how he had felt after moving in with Jerome and getting his job as a mason. This feeling, however, was even more intense.

"I'll convince him," Stanton stated confidently. He gripped Francois's hips and pushed him up the bed. As Stanton grabbed the lube, he explained, "The only other person Jerome loves is his brother. Tony moved to Wisconsin a year and a half ago for an awesome job opportunity." Crawling onto the bed, Stanton pushed between Francois's legs, appreciating how his lover didn't resist. "Jerome would have moved out there when Tony did, but he didn't want to leave me behind, and I couldn't find a position out there."

Gods, I have a lover.

As Stanton peered down and admired Francois's lean, toned form, he skimmed his palm up his thigh. "Gonna suck you now while I open you up for my dick." His left hand reached Francois's groin, and he carefully cupped his balls. Remembering how he'd liked it when he squeezed them, he did it now . . . and pride flooded him when Francois moaned. "Yeah, I like that sound."

"J-Just so you know," Francois muttered on panting breaths. "I'm gonna fuck you right back."

Stanton's chute muscles clench, but his gut tightened with anticipation. "Yeah," he agreed, nodding while releasing Francois's ball sack. "Sounds perfect."

After popping the lid of the lube, Stanton poured a liberal amount on the fingers of his right hand. "I've never done this, but I watched some porn and did some reading," he admitted, closing the lid with his thumb. "Let me know if I do something wrong."

"I-I know I will love it," Francois told him. "Because it's you."

Stanton's stomach twisted for a whole different reason, and something fluttered in his chest. Peering at Francois, he couldn't find any words to respond. When the slender vampire just smiled at him, Stanton smiled back.

"Now, my beloved," Francois urged, lifting his legs, grabbing the backs of his thighs, and spreading himself. "Do what you wish wiz me."

Heeding Francois's words, Stanton dropped the tube of lube and reached down with his other hand. He pressed his slicked fingertips to the vampire's hole, then eased one inside. Feeling the squeeze on his finger, he groaned softly, and his erection twitched.

Stanton's heart hammered in his chest as he pulled his finger nearly free, then pushed it back in again. He stared raptly at where he fingered Francois, having never seen anything so sexy in his life. When he pushed in a second finger beside the first, he crooked them a little and—

Francois moaned and rocked into his touch. "More, my beloved," he encouraged. "Faster."

Obeying, Stanton pulled his fingers out, then pushed them back in. When he pegged Francois's prostate again, the twitching of his lover's erection caught his attention. He saw the pre-cum bubble up from the slit, and his desire to taste slammed through him anew.

Planting his weight on his left hand, Stanton bent over. He opened his mouth and wrapped his lips around Francois's crown. While swiping his tongue over the flared head, he suckled lightly on the bobbing flesh.

Francois's lightly flavored pre-cum teased his taste buds pleasantly. That combined with the taste of Francois's smooth skin, causing a craving for more. He sucked harder as he sank down a little, massaging the length in his mouth with his tongue.

At the same time, Stanton began working Francois's chute in earnest. He spread his fingers a little and twisted them, massaging and stretching the muscular channel. Petting his prostate often, Stanton moaned at the nearly steady flow of pre-cum dripping onto his tongue.

Balancing carefully on his knees, he cradled Francois's testicles as he worked in a third finger.

Francois groaned and shuddered. "S-So close," he warned gruffly. His cock twitched within the confines of Stanton's mouth. "Stanton!"

Stanton felt Francois's hand on his head, pushing at him gently. Peering up at Francois, he ignored the warning. Instead, he sank as far as he could on his lover's erection—which was only about halfway—and at the same time, pressed firmly against his prostate.

To Stanton's delight, Francois's eyes widened, his jaw sagged open, and a deep moan rumbled from him. He also orgasmed. While Francois's eyes rolled to the back of his head, he flooded Stanton's waiting mouth with his seed.

Swallowing swiftly, Stanton hummed in surprised pleasure. Francois's cum coated his taste buds deliciously. He wanted more . . . so much more, and sucked and swallowed greedily.

Then, remembering the advice he'd read online, Stanton used Francois's relaxed orgasmic state to push a fourth finger into his vampire's chute. He was a big man, and he didn't want to hurt his smaller lover. Even though Francois's dick stopped spurting, he didn't soften, filling Stanton with pride.

Stanton eased off Francois's erection, his own cock's throbbing twitches flooding him with driving need. He needed like he never had before. Slipping his fingers free of Francois's channel, Stanton gripped himself. He grabbed the lube and added some more.

Stanton levered over Francois and guided his crown to Francois's greased hole. When he touched himself to his lover, he froze and peered up at him. "Should I put on a condom?"

Why didn't I think about that before?

Francois met his gaze with a loopy smile. "No, my beloved." He released his thighs and wrapped them around Stanton's waist. "No condoms between us."

A shiver of excitement trickled down Stanton's spine. Giving in to his body's need, he pushed . . . hard. When his bulbous crown popped past Francois's guardian muscle, he gasped. The exquisite heat and pressure went straight to his head . . . and his balls . . . and he thrust, sinking as deep as he could go. Stanton bucked, pulling partway out, then jerked forward again.

With his senses on fire with pleasure, Stanton couldn't have stopped it if he'd even realized it was so close. One pump, two, and he froze as a cry of delight burst from his throat. Shuddering above Francois, he flooded his vampire with his seed.

CHAPTER TWELVE

Francois cracked an eyelid, uncertain what had woken him. With the marathon he and Stanton had enjoyed, he should have been damn near in a coma. After Stanton had apologized for coming embarrassingly fast, Francois had explained how flattered he was that his human had lost all control.

Damn heady stuff.

"Besides," Francois had added. "It's not as if we are anywhere near being done."

Then Francois had grabbed the damp towel from the floor—he'd guessed Stanton had used it to dry off after his shower earlier—and had cleaned them up. Using the teasing as foreplay, he'd begun another round. Mounting Stanton and completing their bond had been one of the highlights of Francois's life . . .and he intended to do it over and over for centuries.

So what woke me?

The soft murmur of the TV could still be heard from the other room, telling Francois that Jerome was probably still passed out in there. In fact, he could hear the human's snores. As Francois parsed out the other noises of the apartment complex, he realized there was an odd popping and cracking noise that he couldn't place.

It reminded him of the noises a shifter's body made when they changed forms.

Then . . . Francois smelled it.

Smoke!

What zee hell?

Francois eased out of Stanton's bed. Being the little spoon would take some getting used to, but he loved how it felt to have his big human's arms wrapped around him. Plus, it seemed to make Stanton happy. Once his beloved had accepted their connection, he'd turned into a very touchy-feely guy.

I hope he's zat way out of zee house, too.

Time would tell.

After grabbing his jeans, Francois jerked them on. As he zipped, he crossed to the door. He opened it, and a fresh wave of smoke hit his nostrils, and his eyes stung a little.

"Oh fuck," Francois cried, pivoting and sprinting back to the bed. He shook Stanton's shoulder. "Wake up, beloved," he urged. "We have a problem."

"Hmmm?" Stanton turned his head and peered up at him blearily. "Wassit?"

"Zere's a fire somewhere around here, Stanton," Francois told him. "We need to find it and put it out or get out of here. Get dressed." The pop of something electrical exploding not too far away reached his ears. "Probably just get out of here. Come on."

Francois grabbed his shirt and tugged it on as he pushed his bare feet into his shoes, skipping his socks. To his relief, his cell phone was still in his pocket. As he yanked it free, Francois was pleased to see Stanton up and moving.

"I'm going to check on Jerome and see if I can figure out where zee fire is," Francois told Stanton. "Hurry, beloved."

After Stanton had nodded and returned to pulling on clothes, Francois rushed from the room. He squinted against the light smoke filling the air. When he reached the end of the hall, Francois groaned. The wall near the kitchen licked with flames, and if he had to guess, it was the sound of breaking glass that had roused him, since the small window over the sink had shattered.

Francois jogged in the other direction, toward the flickering light of the TV. Rounding the sofa, he peered at Jerome. The human was still snoring, passed out in the recliner.

Gripping the human's shoulder, Francois shook it. "Wake up, Jerome," he ordered, uncomfortable with the heat at his back. Using the phone in his other hand, he called nine-one-one. "Jerome!" he cried, trying again. "Wake up!"

When the operator picked up, Francois rattled off Stanton's address and the situation.

Stanton lumbered into the room and hurried over to him. Instead of trying to help him wake Jerome, Stanton slid his arms under his friend's body and hefted him into his arms. He started toward the door.

"Let's get out of here." Stanton then jutted his chin in the direction of a bookshelf. "Grab Billy."

Francois followed his gaze and realized his beloved must have been referring to his beta fish. Nodding, he continued to talk to the operator, although there wasn't much else to tell her. He tucked the fish's container under his arm so he had a hand to open the apartment door before starting down the stairs. It wasn't until he'd reached the lawn and he'd turned around that he saw the graffiti sprayed across Stanton and Jerome's door and the side of the building.

Faggots deserve death!

"Good grief," Stanton muttered, having obviously spotted the hateful words. Shaking his head, he placed Jerome on the lawn. "I'm gonna go pound on the doors of my neighbors."

Biting back a growl, Francois nodded. As he explained the graffiti to the operator, who said responders were on their way, he watched Stanton begin to pound on the nearest doors. Francois ached to be right there beside him, but he resisted, knowing Stanton wouldn't understand.

I will watch carefully and be patient.

Instead, Francois began sweeping the area. If the fire starter was still around, he or she couldn't be pleased that their targets had escaped the apartment unharmed.

Who zee hell would do zis?

Deciding making another call was more important than tying up the operator, Francois hit the end button. He swiftly dialed Rhyme. If he'd been home, he would have contacted his coven second, but he didn't feel he had that right here.

"It's the middle of the night, Francois," Rhyme grumbled. "What the hell is it?"

"Someone set Stanton and Jerome's apartment building on fire," Francois stated bluntly. "Zere was a slur painted on zeir door. I zink Stanton was zee target."

As Francois spoke, he searched out his beloved once more. When he didn't see him right away, he scowled. The sirens in the distance, coupled with the roar of the growing fire, made shouting for him pointless.

"We're on our way, and I'll notify the inner circle," Rhyme told him.

"Zank you." Distracted, Francois disconnected the call.

"My god. What happened?" Jerome asked, sounding groggy.

"Apartment fire," Francois replied quickly, his gaze still focused on the apartment building. He placed the small aquarium holding the beta beside Jerome's hip. "Are you okay by yourself?"

Although, technically, Jerome wouldn't be alone. Some of the neighbors were now milling around the area. Couples and families held each other. Singles hugged themselves while pressing their phones to their ears.

"I'm good, man," Jerome told him. "Where's Stanton?"

"He was helping to clear zee building," Francois told him. "I need to go find him."

Francois didn't wait for Jerome's response. Jogging toward the corner where he thought his beloved had rounded, he searched the area. The flames were heavier on that side, and

Francois guessed that was where whoever had started the fire.

"Stanton?" Francois called, even though he doubted it would do any good. He spotted an open door with smoke pouring from it and headed that way. "Stanton?"

Please tell me he didn't go inside.

Francois tried to scent his beloved, but his vampire senses were muddled by the thick smoke. Trusting his gut, the sixth sense that told him his kind human would indeed try to help someone, he put his hand over his mouth and nose and headed inside. From the location of the apartment and how heavy the smoke and flames were, Francois guessed the place was located directly beneath Stanton and Jerome's place.

To his relief, Francois immediately spotted Stanton bent over a chair in the living room.

Hurrying to Stanton's side, Francois realized he was helping a little old lady to her feet. The problem seemed to be the cat in her arms, which was doing its best to get away — probably to hide. The woman couldn't handle the cat and keep her balance.

"Stanton, come on," Francois cried, drawing his attention.

"Misses Beaterman needs to get Muffy in his crate," Stanton told him around a couple of coughs. "But she can't remember where his crate is."

Francois nodded. "Okay. I can help." He grabbed the cat's nape and lifted it from the older lady's arms while hazing his eyes. When she looked up at him and gasped, he knew she was shocked at the sight of his blood-red irises. "Where is your cat carrier?" Francois demanded softly, delving into her mind.

Francois snagged a memory just as she replied, "In the coat closet."

Of course it is.

Then Francois planted the idea that the red in his eyes was just a trick of the light before releasing her mind.

Still holding the cat by its nape, Francois hustled to the closet near the front door. He hissed at the heat of the knob when he turned it but ignored the pain. Yanking the door open, he immediately spotted the carrier on the floor.

Francois snagged the carrier, then eased the cat inside and shut the door. By the time he lifted the caged cat, Stanton had urged Misses Beaterman to her feet, and they were heading toward him. Turning toward the door, Francois froze.

A muscular brunette stood there holding a gun, smiling at them. "When you escaped your apartment before my fire could reach it, I was so pissed." Her smile turned malicious. "This is so much better. A coupla fags dying while trying to save an old lady's cat. How dumb can you be?"

"Esmerelda, did you start this fire?" Stanton snapped angrily, as he took a step toward her.

"Of course, I did." The woman—Esmerelda—swung the gun and pointed it at Stanton. "Back up, Stan," she ordered coldly. "You deserve what's coming to you for getting Anthony and Benjamin fired like that."

"I didn't—" Stanton started, but a crash behind them drowned out his words.

Francois took advantage of the distraction. Lunging forward, he grabbed her wrist and shoved it upward. The weapon fired, and Francois felt a sting to his shoulder, but he ignored it.

Using his momentum and vampire strength, Francois shoved Esmerelda out of the way. "Get out here, Stanton," he roared as he continued to propel her backward. He cleared the sidewalk and made it to the lawn just as his sensitive vampire hearing heard the sound of people running toward him.

"Drop the gun!" someone yelled.

At the same time, another person ordered, "Step away from each other and drop the weapon!"

Francois didn't think that was such a good idea, but he

needed to obey law enforcement. No way did he want to get tossed in jail. He had a beloved to care for.

Attempting to obey, Francois swung Esmerelda's arms in an upward arc. He released her and lifted his hands as he backed away. Warily, he watched to see what she would do.

"That man attacked me," Esmerelda claimed as she lowered her weapon. "I was just defending myself."

"That's bullshit, Esmerelda," Stanton countered as he helped Misses Beaterman onto the grass with one arm. In his other hand, he held the cat carrier. "Esmerelda started the fire, officer."

While one officer was disarming Esmerelda of her weapon, the other man glanced between them all as if trying to figure out who was telling the truth.

"These fine young men are telling the truth," Misses Beaterman claimed, her voice a bit raspy from the smoke. "That young woman admitted to starting the fire because these young men are gay, as if who we love has anything to do with anyone else." She clung to Stanton as she continued fiercely, "And she was going to lock us in my apartment and let us burn, making it look like they died trying to save me."

The officer who'd disarmed Esmerelda grabbed her again, and even as she screamed obscenities and how everyone was lying, he cuffed her. "It's just until we can get everything sorted out," the man told Esmerelda, but she continued to struggle and yell. "If you continue to resist, I will be forced to take you in regardless."

That seemed to set Esmerelda off even more, and the officer ended up frog-marching her away.

"I'll need to take everyone's statements. I'm Officer Merlzer." He swept his gaze over them, then added, "Let's get everyone checked first. Can you round the building? Or should I have the paramedics bring a stretcher around?"

"A stretcher would be lovely, Officer Merlzer," Misses

Beaterman replied.

Officer Merlzer used the microphone attached to his shoulder and called for assistance. Paramedics quickly arrived. They helped Misses Beaterman onto the stretcher, and Stanton placed her cat carrier on her stomach.

As soon as Stanton's hands were empty, Francois stepped close. He grabbed his lover's fingers, pleased when his beloved didn't attempt to pull away. Even better, he wrapped his arm around Francois and tucked him close to his side.

Stanton grinned down at him as they started after the others. "Are you always going to cause this much trouble?"

At first, Francois thought Stanton was actually angry. With his sense of smell still overwhelmed by smoke, he couldn't scent him. Then he noticed the twinkle in Stanton's eyes and how the corners of his lips twitched.

Smirking, Francois murmured, "How about I just promise zat your life will never be boring?"

"That'll work," Stanton replied as they rounded the building. Then, right there in front of dozens of neighbors, strangers, and friends, Stanton paused and captured Francois's lips.

As Francois returned Stanton's lip-lock, he rubbed up and down his beloved's spine, reassuring himself that his human was alive, well, and in his arms.

Everyzing else is icing on zee cake.

When Stanton broke the kiss and grinned down at him, uncaring at the wolf whistles that rent the air, Francois realized that, even sweaty, sooty, and filthy, he had never been happier. His beloved had taught him to enjoy the moment, and they would navigate that future together.

YOU MAY ALSO ENJOY THE FOLLOWING FROM EXTASY BOOKS INC:

Capturing Autumn's Airy Breeze
Charlie Richards

Excerpt

Agnoroth knew he'd fucked up.

The story of my life.

The Fates had been laughing at him that day over eight months before. Agnoroth had met his mate—Kristof—the other half of his soul, while helping the fire dragon, Perentian, kidnap the man's friend. The friend—Riley—had been mated to another dragon named Dagskon. Perentian had claimed Dagskon had stolen a valuable gem from him. The plan had been to use Riley as a bargaining chip to get the gem back.

The plan hadn't worked, naturally.

Along the way, Agnoroth had run into his half-brother, Kazeem, who was also mated with one of Kristof's best friends. A human named Stefan. Kazeem had explained the truth of the matter—that Perentian had stolen the gem from the dragon king, and Dagskon had returned it to the king. Once he'd known the truth, Agnoroth had released Riley, but the damage was done.

Kidnapping a mate was a very serious crime.

Agnoroth had been fortunate. Since Kazeem had stood up for him, speaking on his behalf to the king, Agnoroth had been given a reduced sentence. For helping Perentian—even though it'd been under false pretenses and duress—Agnoroth had still served six months in the king's service as a gardener.

He knew Perentian had been put to death, but kidnapping a mate hadn't been his only crime. Fortunately, before the sentence had been carried out, Perentian had revealed where he'd hidden the crystal orb he'd stolen from him. That had been the main reason Agnoroth had agreed to help the dragon. He'd wanted his gem back, so he'd been sympathetic to the fire dragon's desire.

Being an air dragon, Agnoroth hadn't minded the work. He'd used his magick to blow the leaves into piles instead of actually raking. His abilities also made it easy for him to throw gusts of wind at trees to knock off ripe fruit, then guide them into his basket.

While the chores were menial, Agnoroth had found he'd enjoyed them, making his six-month sentence fly by.

Agnoroth stared at the apartment building. "And now I'm here," he mumbled, rubbing the back of his neck. He hadn't revealed who Kristof was to him to anyone. "Time to see if he'll even talk to me."

Tipping his head back, Agnoroth enjoyed the cool autumn breeze caressing his cheeks. He thought about that moment when he'd had Kristof in his arms. Grabbing his mate to stop him from interfering with Perentian had been spine-tingling. The feel of the human's body, even through the thick winter clothes, had caused his dick to swell. A second later, realizing who Kristof was to him and how their first interaction was about to go, Agnoroth had damn near felt his heart break.

So much for making a good first impression, but I'll make him understand.

For the last several weeks, Agnoroth had been watching Kristof's movements. He knew his mate worked as a mechanic and used a motorcycle to commute. The sight of Kristof on his older model *Indian* always caused Agnoroth's blood to heat and his dick to thicken.

Watching from the park bench across the street from the apartments, Agnoroth waited. He glanced at his watch and saw the time was twenty after six. Anticipation began to surge through him.

If Kristof kept with his pattern, he would be home within the next few minutes.

Agnoroth hummed as the sound of Kristof's *Indian* reached his ears. Peering down the road, he watched as his mate appeared. The man's faded jeans molded to his body, showcasing his very fine ass and his long, muscular legs.

As his mouth watered, Agnoroth rose to his feet. He kept his focus on Kristof as he exited the park and headed to the crosswalk. As Agnoroth waited for the light to change, Kristof parked his motorcycle and took off his helmet.

The way Kristof's muscles flexed drew a groan from Agnoroth's throat. He reached down and adjusted his growing erection as he watched Kristof unhook his backpack from the back of the bike. The beep of the crosswalk signal registered, and Agnoroth started swiftly across the street.

By the time Agnoroth reached the other side, Kristof was already heading up his walk toward his apartment building. He continued at a leisurely pace, hoping to reach his mate's door a moment after he'd entered his home. Just before Kristof reached the stairs that led to his third-floor apartment, someone called Kristof's name.

Agnoroth slowed his steps as he watched a tall, muscular blond man jog the last couple of steps to reach Kristof's side. When Kristof turned his attention toward the man, a scowl curved his lips. Kristof's eyes narrowed, and his expression darkened as he took in the man who was an inch taller and just as broad.

"What do you want, Casey?" Kristof asked, stepping back when the man — Casey — tried to reach out and touch him.

Casey smiled widely as he swept his gaze over Kristof in what was clearly a hungry manner. "Aww, don't sound like that, Kristof," Casey all but purred in a deep rumble. "You've been avoiding my calls, so I had to come by." Once again, Casey stepped closer and reached for Kristof, resting his palm on his leather-jacket-covered arm. "I've missed you."

Kristof growled softly as he turned, pulling away. "I told you we were through, Casey," he stated, his tone beyond cold. "Take off."

"You don't mean that," Casey cried, grabbing at his arm again.

"I do mean that," Kristof countered, half-turning to face him. "All I wanted was fidelity, and you couldn't give me that, so we're through."

Casey's lecherous expression disappeared as his eyes narrowed. His features took on a hard look. "You went away for two weeks without telling me. That wasn't my fault," he declared. "Besides, it was just a blowjob." Casey scoffed. "I don't even know how you found out about it in the first place."

"How I found out is beside the point," Kristof growled. "And I did tell you. Now, let go of me before I—"

"Before you what?" Casey demanded, his blue eyes flashing with anger. "You gonna hit me, Kris?" His lip curled as he leaned close. "You're not into that, *remember*? *I* am, and if you think for a second that you get to decide to walk away from me before I'm done with you, then—"

"Then you should listen to Kristof and walk away," Agnoroth declared, unable to stand by and watch his mate be manhandled. By the time he finished speaking, Agnoroth had reached their side. "Release him now."

Casey didn't obey. Instead, he pinned Agnoroth with a scathing look. "Keep walkin', fem," he ordered, sneering. "You don't wanna get involved in this."

Agnoroth ignored the insult—*fem*, short for effeminate. He'd heard it before. Due to the fact that he was an air dragon, his voice in human form came out a surprisingly high tenor.

That didn't bother him.

What bothered him was the fact that Casey wasn't obeying.

Fighting back his desire to unleash his claws and tear into the asshole human, Agnoroth narrowed his eyes and hissed, "I'm already involved."

Kristof's gasp drew both men's attention. His mate's dark eyes appeared wide, betraying his shock. Even his face began to pale.

Damn. Not the reaction I was hoping for.

Oh, wait. That's a flush. And did he just glance toward my groin?

Nice!

ABOUT THE AUTHOR

Charlie started writing fantasy when she was eight, and after stumbling onto her first erotic romance at age nineteen, she realized her true calling. She now focuses on writing gay erotic romance, normally of the paranormal variety, with heroes of all kinds. With the help and support of her husband, Charlie finally fulfilled one of her life-long goals . . . move to acreage with her horses. You can often find her curled up with her laptop and a cup of tea or glass of wine, creating her next adventure. Charlie enjoys exploring the mountains of her new Oregon home on horseback, 4-wheeler, or motorcycle.

She can be reached at ch.richards2010@yahoo.com
Or visit her at www.charlie-richards.com

www.ingramcontent.com/pod-product-compliance
Lightning Source LLC
Chambersburg PA
CBHW070508130626
46555CB00003B/1200